Monsieur Pamplemousse and the Secret Mission

Michael Bond

G.K.HALL &CO.
Boston, Massachusetts
1991

Published in Large Print by arrangement with
Hodder and Stoughton, Ltd.

G.K. Hall Large Print Book Series.

Set in 16 pt. Plantin.

Library of Congress Cataloging-in-Publication Data

Bond, Michael.
    Monsieur Pamplemousse and the secret mission / Michael
Bond.
      p.   cm. — (G.K. Hall large print book series)
    ISBN 0-8161-5110-5
    1. Large type books. I. Title.
    [PR6052.O52M68   1991]
    823′.914—dc20   90-44633

——1——

Dinner with the Director

'PAMPLEMOUSSE, I HAVE to tell you, and I say this not simply in my capacity as your commander-in-chief, Director of *Le Guide*, the greatest gastronomic publication in all France, but also, I trust, as a friend and confidant; we are, at this very moment, sitting on a *bombe à retardement*. A *bombe* which could, moreover, explode at any moment.'

Having delivered himself at long last of a matter that had clearly been exercising his mind for most of the evening, the Director sat back in his chair with a force which, had his words been taken literally, might well have triggered off the mechanism and blown them both to Kingdom Come. As it was he took advantage of the finding of a piece of white cotton on the lapel of his dinner jacket in order to study the effect his pronouncement had made on his audience of one.

He eyed Monsieur Pamplemousse with

1

some concern. Normally Monsieur Pample-mousse managed to retain an air of unruf-fled calm no matter what the situation. It was a habit he had acquired during his years working as a detective for the Paris Sûreté, when to show the slightest spark of emotion would have been taken by others as a sign of weakness. But for once he appeared to have lost this valuable faculty. His features were contorted out of all recognition and he seemed to be fighting to avoid losing control of himself altogether before finally disap-pearing under the dining-room table.

The Director jumped to his feet. 'Are you unwell, Aristide? I assure you, it was not my intention to cause alarm. I merely . . .'

Monsieur Pamplemousse struggled back into a sitting position, regaining his com-posure in an instant. The mask slipped back into place as if it had never left his face.

'Forgive me, Monsieur.' He mopped his brow with a napkin. 'I don't know what came over me.'

The fact of the matter was he'd been searching under the table for his right shoe. It had become detached from its appropriate foot earlier in the evening under circum-stances best left unexplained to his host, and he'd been taking advantage of the other's preoccupation with his problems in the hope of solving one of his own.

The Director looked relieved. 'I feel you may have been overworking lately, Pamplemousse. Too much work and no play. Perhaps,' he added meaningly, 'a rest of some kind might be in order? A spell in some quiet, out of the way place for a while.'

He reached across to an occasional table and lifted the lid of a small satinwood-lined silver cigar box. 'Can I tempt you?'

'Thank you, Monsieur, but no.' Monsieur Pamplemousse picked up his glass and passed it gently to and fro just below his nose, swirling the remains of the wine as he did so, savouring the aroma with the accustomed ease of one to whom such an action was as natural as the breathing in of the air around him. It was a noble wine, a wine of great breeding; a Chambertin, Clos de Bèze, '59. He wondered if the Director made a habit of drinking such classic wines with his meals or whether he wanted some favour that only he, Pamplemousse, could provide. Suspecting the latter, he decided to pay more attention to what was being said.

'It is necessary that I protect my olfactory nerves, Monsieur,' he added primly.

'Nerves which, like my taste buds, are on duty day and night in the service of *Le Guide;* selecting and savouring, accepting and rejecting . . .'

'Yes, yes, Pamplemousse . . .' The Director snipped the end off his Corona with a gesture of impatience. 'I am fully aware of your dedication to duty and of your total incorruptibility. Those qualities are, if I may say so, two of the main reasons why I invited you and Madame Pamplemousse to dine with us tonight.'

The implication that perhaps they were the only two reasons was not lost on Monsieur Pamplemousse, but he accepted the underlying rebuke without rancour. Had he been totally honest there was nothing he would have liked better than to round off the meal with a cigar; especially one of a more modest nature than his host had chosen. In his experience large cigars tended to lose their appeal halfway through, when they either went out or the end became too soggy for comfort. A slim panatella would have been ideal. He felt his mouth begin to water at the thought. However, with his annual increment due in a little less than a month there was no harm in sacrificing the

4

pleasure to be derived from inhaling smoke in exchange for a few bonus points.

'Apart from which,' he added, 'Madame Pamplemousse does not like the smell of tobacco fumes in my clothes.'

'Ah!' The Director's voice held a wealth of understanding. 'Wives, Pamplemousse! Wives!' He paused before applying the flame of a match to his cigar. 'Would Madame Pamplemousse rather *I* didn't?'

'Of course not, Monsieur.' Monsieur Pamplemousse refrained from embarking on a tedious explanation of his wife's ability to distinguish between smoke which came through self-indulgence and smoke which was acquired second-hand. The former attracted a sniff full of accusation, the latter a snort which merely expressed disgust.

Instead he sat back, wishing his host would get on with the business in hand rather than continue to beat about the bush. That there was something on his mind was clear. Equally, it must be a matter too delicate to be discussed in the office. The Director didn't normally invite members of his staff, however valued, to his home. That it was something he did not wish to talk about in the presence of either his own wife or Doucette, was equally apparent. Several times during the meal there had been a gap in the conversation; sometimes an uneasily long gap, but each time it had been neatly plugged by an abrupt change of subject, rather as if the Director, like the chairman of a television chat show, had armed himself with a list of topics to cover every eventuality.

Talk over the fish soufflé—a delightfully airy concoction containing a *poisson* he didn't immediately recognise—had been devoted to the future of the E.E.C. The *gigot d'agneau*, done in the English manner with roast potatoes, peas and mint jelly, had come and gone over a discourse ranging from the price of eggs to the iniquities of the tax collector. The fact that the dish had been accompanied by a strange yellow substance, like a kind of thick pancake, had gone unremarked—and in the case of Madame Pamplemousse, who had a naturally suspicious nature, uneaten. It had been overshadowed by talk of the history of clocks and the invention of the fusee mechanism of regulation by means of a conical pulley wheel, a subject on which the Director was something of an expert.

The cheese and the sweet—a totally entrancing syllabub, again done in the English way using sherry rather than white wine, had triggered off a long monologue from the Director about his early days on the Paris Bourse.

At the end of the meal, the *petits fours* reduced to less than half their original number, the coffee cups drained, the Director, with an almost audible note of relief in his voice, drew breath long enough to suggest that perhaps Madame Pamplemousse would like a tour of the house. Madame Pamplemousse had been only too pleased. Madame Pamplemousse, in fact, could hardly wait. She had been on the edge of her seat ever since they arrived.

It was the kind of house that many people dream of, but relatively few set foot in, let alone achieve. Situated on the edge of a small forest, it was less than thirty kilometres from Paris, yet it could have been a million miles away. Mullioned windows looked out onto gardens of a neatness which could only have been brought about by the constant attention of many hands over the centuries; not a blade of grass was out of place, not a flower ever shed its petals unnoticed. He was glad he had parked his car with its exhaust pipe facing away from the shrubbery.

Beyond the gardens lay orchards and fields in which corn grew and sheep could be seen grazing peacefully within the boundary walls, their concentration undisturbed by any sound other than those made by passing birds en route for sunnier climes or bees going about their endless work. In its day it must have been even more remote and self-contained, well able to live off its own fat.

It was a tranquil scene, as unlike his own flat in the eighteenth arrondissement of Paris as it was possible to imagine. Doucette would be in her element; so, for that matter, would Pommes Frites, who'd taken advantage of the moment to go off on his own voyage of exploration. He'd seemed in rather a hurry and Monsieur Pamplemousse hoped he was behaving himself. Habits acquired in the streets of Montmartre, where every tree and every lamp-post received its full quota of attention, would not go down well in such gracious surroundings. Alarm bells would sound.

Alone at last, he sat back awaiting the moment of truth, but the Director was not to be hurried. Putting off the evil moment yet again, he reached for a bell push.

'I'm sure you won't say "no" to an Armagnac, Aristide. I have some of your favourite—a '28 Réserve d'Artagnon.'

Not for the first time Monsieur Pamplemousse found himself marvelling at the other's knowledge and attention to detail. Such thoughtfulness! Nineteen twenty-eight— the year of his birth. Beneath the somewhat aloof exterior there was an incisive mind at work—cataloguing information, sorting and storing it for future use as and when required. Unless . . . He stiffened; unless the Director had had his file out for some reason!

His thoughts were broken into by a knock on the door.

'*Entrez!*'

Monsieur Pamplemousse glanced up. Had a butler entered bearing balloon glasses and bottle on a silver salver he would not have been unduly surprised. An elderly retainer, perhaps, kept on in the family despite his advancing years, because that was the way it had always been and because his wife, an apple-cheeked octogenarian from Picardy, would not be parted from her stove. That would account for a certain Englishness in the meal.

What he didn't expect to see framed in the doorway was a figure of such loveliness and roundness and juxtapositioning of roundnesses, each vying one with the other for pride of place, it momentarily took his breath away and nearly caused him to slip back under the table again.

'Ah, Elsie,' the Director turned in his chair. 'A glass of the Réserve d'Artagnon for our guest. I think perhaps I will join him with a cognac; the Grande Champagne.'

Monsieur Pamplemousse watched in a dream as the apparition wiggled its way to a marble-topped side cabinet on the far side of the room and bent down to open one of the lower doors.

He closed his eyes and then opened them again, allowing the figure to swim into view and place two large glasses on the table in front of him, before clasping the bottle to her bosom in order to withdraw the cork.

'Say when.' The voice came as a surprise. Somehow it didn't go with the body.

Half expecting one of the three musketeers depicted on the label to wink back at him, he focused his gaze on two large round eyes of a blueness that beggared description. Lowering his gaze slightly in an effort to escape them he found himself peering into a valley of such lushness and depth it only

10

served to emphasise the delights of mentally scaling the mountainous slopes on either side to reach their all too visible cardinal points. A voice which he barely recognised as his own and which seemed to come from somewhere far away, tardily repeated the word 'when'.

'Thank you, Elsie. That was an excellent meal. I'm sure Monsieur Pamplemousse will agree, won't you, Aristide?'

Monsieur Pamplemousse cleared his throat. 'Stock Pot material,' he said, not to be outdone in gallantry. The lamb had been a trifle overdone for his taste, the merest soupçon, but that was a minor criticism. Had he been on duty reporting on the meal for *Le Guide*, he would most certainly have recommended the chef for a Stock Pot.

'Forgive my asking, but the cake which accompanied the lamb . . .'

'Koik!' Elsie's eyes narrowed as she fixed him with a withering look. 'That's not koik. That's Yorkshire puddin', innit.'

'Ah!' Monsieur Pamplemousse sank back into his chair feeling suitably ashamed of himself, his copy-book blotted. So that was the famous pudding from Yorkshire he had heard so much about. It had been a memorable experience, an eye-opener. He

11

looked at her with new respect. 'Is it one of your recipes?'

' 'course.'

'Perhaps,' he ventured, oblivious to a disapproving grunt on his right, 'perhaps you could show me how to make it one day? With Monsieur le Directeur's approval, of course.'

Elsie gave a giggle as she crossed to the door. 'Saucebox!' She jerked a thumb in the direction of his host. 'You're worse than what 'e is and that's saying something. See you later,' she added meaningly.

The Director shifted uneasily in the silence which followed Elsie's departure.

'Nothing in this life is wholly perfect, Pamplemousse,' he said at last. 'A nice girl, but she has a strange way of expressing herself. I imagine it has something to do with the difference in the English education system.'

Monsieur Pamplemousse looked thoughtful. There were times when he wondered about the Director.

His thoughts were read and analysed in an instant. 'She also suffers a great deal from *mal de tête*. You wouldn't think so to look at her, but I have never known a girl so given to headaches.'

Monsieur Pamplemousse cupped the glass of Armagnac in his hands. It was dark with age. The fumes were powerful and heady. There was a velvety fire to it which would cling to the side of the glass for many days to come.

'*C'est la vie*, Monsieur!'

'The trouble is I took her in to oblige a friend. She is learning the language and she came over to do her practicals—there was some kind of domestic trouble—it's all rather embarrassing. I engaged her out of sheer kindness, hoping she would help the children with their English, but it hasn't worked out. They say they have difficulty in understanding her. Rapport is low. She will have to go, of course. My wife does not approve.'

'Wives, Monsieur,' sighed Monsieur Pamplemousse. 'Wives!'

He could hardly blame her. It was difficult to imagine Doucette allowing him to be alone in the kitchen with Elsie for five minutes, let alone accept her as part of the ménage. Wherever she went there would be trouble with the distaff side.

'What particularly grieves me is that in the meantime I have discovered she is possessed of a hidden talent. A God-given

13

gift—and at its highest level, Pample-mousse, it *is* a God-given gift—she cooks like an angel; an angel from heaven, without help, without recourse to recipe books . . .'

Monsieur Pamplemousse nearly choked on his Armagnac. 'You mean . . . she cooked the meal this evening? Not just the pudding from Yorkshire, but the *entire* meal?'

The Director nodded.

'Including these exquisite *petits fours?*'

'*Especially* the *petits fours.* "Afters", she calls them. They are one of her specialities. That and a dish called "Spotted Dick". She has a great predilection for Spotted Dick.

'I tell you, Pamplemousse, her departure will cause me untold grief. Such talent should not be let go to waste, but unless I find someone to take her in soon I fear the worst. She has only to meet the wrong person, someone less scrupulous than you or I, and poof!' The Director left the rest to the imagination. 'With a figure like that the pressures must be enormous. Even some kind of temporary shelter would be better than nothing.'

Monsieur Pamplemousse felt his mind racing on ahead of him. Things were beginning to fall into place. The reason for the unexpected invitation to dinner. What was it the Director had said earlier? *We* are sitting on a time bomb, Pamplemousse. And what of the strange incident during the meal? The cause of his losing a shoe.

It had happened soon after the entrée. Having decided that the oak, splat-back chairs had been chosen more with an eye to matching the Louis XV refectory table than to their comfort, which was minimal, he had taken advantage of a momentary lull between courses to stretch out his right leg which was in great danger of going to sleep. Almost immediately he wished he hadn't for it encountered another leg, apparently doing the same thing. At first he thought it was an accident and would have apologised to the owner of its opposite number had the Director not once again been in full flight.

A moment later he'd felt a soft but undeniably persistent pressure on the top of his shoe. Then, seconds later, after a half-hearted attempt at withdrawal, there had been another even more persistent squeeze; a sortie from the opposite side of the table from which retreat was impossible. Then came the mounting of the shoe by a toe, a toe which had wriggled its way upward and over the tongue towards his ankle. Soon afterwards it had been joined by a second toe and within moments, so great was the onslaught, so totally irresistible, it began to feel as though there were many more than two toes at work; a whole regiment of toes in fact, gripping and caressing, squeezing and embracing.

A quick glance at Doucette had assured him that all was well. True, she was wearing her pained expression, but that was not unusual. Her attention appeared to be centred wholly on her host.

So, too, was that of the Director's wife. He had to marvel at the duplicity of women. No one would have thought from the rapt expression on her face that her mind was on anything other than her husband, and that other things were going on, or as matters turned out coming off, under cover of the table. In a matter of moments his shoe had parted company with his foot, pushed to one side in order to facilitate an exploratory reconnaissance of his lower calf.

Clearly there were undercurrents at work in the Director's household. Undreamed of depths yet to be plumbed.

Suddenly, he came back to earth with a bump, aware of a silence. A question had been posed; an answer was awaited.

'We have only a small flat, Monsieur,' he began, 'and Madame Pamplemousse is not, I fear, the most understanding of persons when it comes to such matters. Besides, there is Pommes Frites to be considered. He is somewhat set in his ways. I doubt if he will take kindly to moving out of the spare room . . .'

He tried to picture Doucette sharing her kitchen with Elsie, but try as he might he couldn't bring it into any kind of focus.

'Pamplemousse,' the Director had assumed his slow, ponderous voice; the one he reserved for children and idiots. 'I am not asking you to share your flat with anyone. That is not at all what I have in mind. Besides, I doubt if anything short of an earthquake will move Tante Louise.'

Monsieur Pamplemousse felt a certain dizziness. He wondered if he had heard aright. Perhaps the Armagnac was a mistake; he should have said 'when' earlier.

'You doubt if anything short of an earthquake will move Tante Louise, Monsieur?' he repeated, playing for time.

'Does the name St. Georges-sur-Lie mean anything to you, Pamplemousse?'

'St. Georges-sur-Lie? Is it not somewhere in the Loire region? Not far from Saumur?'

Why did the words ring a faint but persistent bell in the back of his mind? He had a feeling he'd heard the name mentioned only recently. Someone in the office had been talking about it.

He closed his eyes, glad to be on safe ground again. The Loire, cradle of French literature and cuisine. The Loire, where they spoke the purest French. He had come to know it relatively late in life. In his younger days he had avoided the area because of the picture it conjured up; all those coachloads of tourists with their cameras. The loss had been his.

'I see *asperges* pickers at work in the fields; *champignons* grown in caves that were hollowed out in the cliffs along the river bank in the days when the great Châteaux were being built; I see walnuts and honey, *pâté* from Chartres, *rillettes* and *rillons* made from pigs raised in Angers . . .'

Getting into his stride now that he was on his own territory, confident that his recollections couldn't fail to be a plus when it came to increment time, Monsieur Pamplemousse gave full rein to his imagination. 'I see freshwater fish too; perch and barbel, poached and served with *beurre blanc*; *matelotes* made with eel caught in the Loire itself; I see *tarte tatin* and pastry shells made of *pâte sucrée*—a layer of pastry cream flavoured with liqueur, then filled with apricots or peaches, ripe and freshly picked, the colour of a maiden's blush, still warm with the sun's rays and decorated with almonds . . .'

He paused for a moment as the memory of an almond-filled tart he'd bought one Sunday morning after Mass in Pitheriens came flooding back.

'There is a small restaurant in Azay-le-Rideau where they serve a most delicious *Gigot de Poulette au pot au feu*. It goes well with the *Bourgueil* of the region. Michelin have given them a star; perhaps it deserves another visit. A reappraisal. I would be happy . . .'

'Forget all that, Pamplemousse.' The Director's unfeeling voice cut across his musings like a hot knife through butter. 'Close your eyes again and consider instead a small hotel in St. Georges-sur-Lie. An hotel where they serve pastry so hard it would tax the ingenuity of a woodpecker. *Bœuf* so overdone it would bring a gleam to the eye of a cobbler awaiting delivery of his next consignment of leather, and *îles flottantes* so heavy they make a mockery of the very name as they sink to the bottom of the dish.'

The Director's words had the desired effect. He remembered now where he had heard the name. One of his colleagues— Duval from Lyons—had been reminiscing and had described how he'd broken a tooth while staying there. It had given rise to much mirth at the time. Madame Grante in Accounts had had to retire to the *Dames*.

'Does it have a mention in Michelin?'

'Nothing. Not even a red rocking chair, although God knows you couldn't find a quieter spot.'

'Gault Millau?'

'They gave it a black toque two years ago and then promptly dropped it. It hasn't appeared since.'

'And no others?'

'There was a brief mention in a guide published by one of the English motoring organisations. I believe they awarded it five stars. But even they seem to have had second thoughts.

'Strictly speaking it should be Bernard's territory this year, but as you know he is not available for the time being.'

'How is Bernard, Monsieur? It was a bit of a shock.'

'Still waters, Pamplemousse. Still waters.'
The Director reached for the cognac. 'He is tending his roses in Mortagne-au-Perche awaiting trial. He denies everything, of course, but I understand his wife has left him. It is all most unfortunate. Rather like your affair with those chorus girls, only not on such a grand scale. I am having to pull strings.' He seemed anxious to change the subject.

Monsieur Pamplemousse stirred uneasily in his chair. He always felt worried when the Director brought up the matter of his early retirement from the Sûreté. It was usually a prelude to some kind of demand; a reminder that but for *Le Guide* he, too, might be tending his roses.

'Perhaps, Monsieur,' he began, 'a visit from your good self would put an end to speculation . . .'

The Director gave a shudder. For some reason the words seemed to have struck home.

'That, Pamplemousse, is the very last thing that must happen.'

'Forgive me, Monsieur, but given all the facts as you have related them to me, I cannot see why . . .'

The Director put a finger to his lips.

'Walls, Pamplemousse, walls!' Crossing swiftly to the door he opened it and peered outside to make sure no one was listening, then turned back into the room. In the time it took him to complete the operation he seemed to have aged considerably, like a man possessed of a great weight on his shoulders.

'The Hôtel du Paradis in St. Georges-sur-Lie,' he said gloomily, 'is owned by my wife's aunt Louise.

'It is a problem beside which the one with Elsie is but a pin prick, a mere drop in the ocean, a passing cloud in the weather map of life.

'As a child I remember some terrible experiences at the hands of her mother with whom I used to go and stay—she was a family friend. She smoked a great deal, which was unusual for a lady in those days, and she had a habit of bathing me with a cigarette in her mouth. The ash used to fall all over me.'

Monsieur Pamplemousse tried to picture the Director sitting in his bath covered in ash and failed miserably.

'Now her daughter, Louise, has inherited the hotel and wishes it to be included in the pages of *Le Guide*. I have told her, the Guide does not work that way, but she refuses to understand.'

Monsieur Pamplemousse considered the matter for a moment or two. 'If that is the only problem,' he said slowly, 'would it not be possible to stretch a point for once? You say that in the past views have been divided. Clearly, there is room for manoeuvre . . .'

'Never!' The word came like a pistol shot.

Monsieur Pamplemousse felt his increment in jeopardy as the Director fixed him with a gimlet stare. '*Le Guide* is like the rock of Gibraltar; immovable, incorruptible. It has always been so and while I am in charge that is how it will remain.'

'I am sorry, Monsieur. I was only trying to be of help.'

'I understand, Aristide. It is good of you. I apologise.' The Director put a hand to his brow. 'But you must understand, *Le Guide* is my life. Suppose we "stretch a point" as you suggest and the connection is discovered. Think what a field day the press would have. The reputation so painstakingly built up over the years and nurtured and cared for, would be gone for ever. The climb upwards can be long and arduous, the fall a matter of seconds.'

'But with respect, Monsieur. She is, after all, your wife's aunt.'

'When things go wrong, Aristide, she is *my* aunt. I cannot afford to take the risk. Remember, too, if *Le Guide* falls, we all fall.'

If the Director had substituted the words 'France falls' for 'we all fall' the effect could hardly have been more dramatic.

Monsieur Pamplemousse fell silent and allowed his gaze to drift out of the window. He was just in time to see his right shoe go past. Or rather, to be strictly accurate, he saw Pommes Frites go past carrying it in his mouth. *Merde!* He bounded to the window and to his horror watched both disappear into the shrubbery at the side of the long driveway. Pommes Frites not only looked as if he was enjoying himself, he wore the confident air of a dog about to bury his favourite bone in a place where no one else would ever find it.

The Director glared at him impatiently as he hobbled back to his seat. 'What *is* the matter with you this evening, Pamplemousse? Are you having trouble with your foot? You seem to be walking in a very strange way all of a sudden.'

'It is nothing, Monsieur. An old war

wound.' It wasn't a total untruth. He had once injured his foot doing rifle drill, bringing the butt down with considerable force on his big toe instead of on the parade ground. It still ached from time to time during inclement weather.

The Director looked suitably chastened. He cleared his throat in lieu of an apology.

'I was about to say, Aristide, it isn't simply a question of *Le Guide*. That in itself would be bad enough, but there is my position in local government to be considered. It is only a minor appointment, but the office carries with it certain advantages. Next year I may be Mayor. One whiff of scandal, and poof! You understand?'

Monsieur Pamplemousse understood all too well. A man in Monsieur le Directeur's position thrived on power. In the end it became a *raison d'être*.

'I am being assailed on all sides, Pamplemousse. Here at home. In the office. The only real peace I have is when I journey between the two and even then the car telephone is always ringing. Yield to Tante Louise and my way of life is in jeopardy. Refuse and it will be made a misery. Either way the outlook is dark.

'Elsie is one problem, but in the end it

will go away; Tante Louise is another matter entirely. When you meet her you will find that in most respects she is a lovely lady; thoughtful and gentle, kind to animals . . . but take my word for it, Pamplemousse, when the female of the species looks you straight in the eye and says "I am only a poor helpless woman, all on my own with no one to turn to for advice and I don't understand these things," watch out!'

'When *I* meet her, Monsieur?' Monsieur Pamplemousse felt his heart sink. He sensed trouble ahead.

The Director drained his glass. 'Pamplemousse, I want you to leave for St. Georges-sur-Lie tomorrow morning. I want you to go there, reconnoitre, make notes and afterwards translate those notes into action. Either the Hôtel du Paradis must be raised above its present abysmal level so that it can be considered for future inclusion in *Le Guide*—and there your expertise will be invaluable—or Tante Louise must be brought to her senses, in which case you will need to draw on your well-known powers of persuasion.

'Take as much time as you like; two weeks . . . three . . . but remember from this moment on you will be on your own.

26

There must be no communication with Headquarters. While you are away your flag will be removed from the map in the Operations Room. You will be visiting a sick aunt in the country; a white lie, but in the circumstances a justifiable one. Tante Louise is undoubtedly sick—no one could be such a diabolical cook and remain in good health. Also, you will be in the country.

'We will meet again on the occasion of your annual interview. I trust you will be the bearer of good news.

'Remember, Pamplemousse, the three A's; *Action*, *Accord* and *Anonymat*. No one outside these four walls must know what is happening.'

Having delivered himself of an address which would have brought a glint of approval to the eyes of General de Gaulle himself had he been alive to hear it, the Director hesitated for a moment as if about to enlarge on the subject. Then, hearing the sound of voices approaching in the corridor outside, he hastily changed his mind.

'Remember Bernard,' he added hurriedly. 'Remember Bernard, and don't let it happen to you. We cannot afford to lose *two* good men in one year.'

'Two?' Monsieur Pamplemousse raised

his eyebrows enquiringly. 'I really do not see . . .'

The Director put a finger to his lips. '*Anonymat*, Pamplemousse,' he hissed as the footsteps stopped outside the door. 'Above all, *anonymat*.'

—2—

A Fruitful Journey

THE JOURNEY HOME was not the happiest in living memory. Whereas a larger, faster car might have coped, the *deux chevaux* was not at its best. The brief given by Monsieur Boulanger to his team of designers when they set about building the first Citroën 2CV was to produce a vehicle for all seasons and all occasions; status and speed were to have low priority. More important was the ability to carry a farmer and his basket of eggs across a ploughed field on a Saturday, allowing him to arrive at market with his wares uncracked, yet have sufficient room to enable him to don his hat and best suit the day after in order to transport his entire family to church. Above all, it had to be cheap and reliable; cheap to buy, cheap to run, and to require the minimum of attention.

Doubtless all the possible permutations such a wide brief encompassed kept Monsieur Boulanger's minions awake for many a night as they added an inch or two here, or mentally removed a superfluous nut and bolt there in a search for a solution which in the end turned out to be both eccentric and ageless.

What none of them probably included in their calculations, bearing in mind that the computer had yet to be invented, and in those days one had to draw the line somewhere, was the possibility of their brainchild being driven by a man wearing only one shoe and with the back seat occupied, not by a basket of eggs, but by a large bloodhound. A bloodhound moreover, who wasn't in the best of moods and who steadfastly refused to co-operate by leaning with the bends, as would most normal passengers, but on the contrary made driving as difficult as possible by putting all his weight very firmly in the opposite direction whenever they tried to negotiate a corner.

Had Monsieur Boulanger envisaged such a possibility he might have extended his original brief, instructing his designers to add a non-slip pad to the accelerator pedal and to modify the otherwise admirable suspension, perhaps even adding a reinforced hand-strap for the benefit of those passengers who, like Madame Pamplemousse, were of a nervous disposition.

As it was, the occupants sat, or rolled about, in complete and utter silence, each busy with their own thoughts. Madame Pamplemousse, her eyes tightly closed, was in a world of her own. Monsieur Pamplemousse, in the few moments when he was able to relax, kept going over the evening's conversation, trying to recall if he had at any time acceded to the Director's request.

The Director had clearly assumed his answer would be in the affirmative—it had been a command rather than a request—but he couldn't remember a point where he'd actually agreed. Certainly the word 'oui' had never passed his lips.

One way and another it had been a strange evening, what with Elsie and then the business with the Director's wife. It needed thinking about.

Pommes Frites' silence was due to the fact that he was in a bit of a huff; a huff which wasn't improved by having to travel in the back of the car. He much preferred sitting in the front alongside his master, even if it did mean wearing a seat belt. At least in the front you could see where you were going rather than where you had been, and you weren't subjected to other indignities.

He stared gloomily out of the rear window at the following traffic, treating the waving and flashing of lights from other late-night revellers with the contempt they deserved. There were times when the behaviour of human beings was totally beyond his comprehension. The same people who would pass him by on the street without so much as a second glance went berserk if they happened to catch sight of him looking out of the back window of Monsieur Pamplemousse's car, pointing at him and nudging each other as if they had never seen a dog before.

As they joined the *Périphérique* at Porte de St. Cloud and entered the tunnel under the Bois de Boulogne, Monsieur Pamplemousse came to a decision. He would make an appointment with the Director first thing in the morning and reject the whole idea. It might not go down too well; his annual increment would be put in jeopardy and the kitchen needed redecorating, but that was too bad. He could hear little warning bells in the back of his mind, bells which all his past experience told him one ignored at one's peril.

The matter decided, the road ahead wide and clear, he settled back in a more relaxed mood.

'You are being very quiet tonight, Doucette,' he ventured, glancing across at his wife. 'Is anything the matter?'

Madame Pamplemousse opened her eyes for a moment and then allowed her hand to rest on his. 'I was thinking. Do you still find me attractive, Aristide?'

Taken aback by this unexpected remark, Monsieur Pamplemousse played for time. 'Of course I do, *chérie*. What a strange question. Why do you ask?'

He received a shy look in return. 'It's just that . . . if you do, I suppose others must too. Earlier this evening I felt someone playing with my foot. It must have been the Director because at the time you were leaning across to pass the wine. I was quite taken aback. I didn't know which way to look.'

Narrowly missing a lorry-load of vegetables on its way to Rungis, Monsieur Pamplemousse changed lanes and negotiated the exit at Porte Dauphine with a sense of outrage. To think, all the time he'd been listening to the Director's ramblings, treating his words like pearls of wisdom, giving them his undivided attention, he was being cuckolded under the table! It only served to confirm his decision. He would definitely *not* be going to St. Georges-sur-Lie. For two pins he would telephone him that very night and tell him so.

Doucette's next words came like a bucket of ice-cold water.

'I think he must have given *you* ideas, Aristide. Perhaps he even made you a little jealous. I saw you reaching out with your foot—and then I felt it too. You haven't behaved as you did this evening since we first went out together. Do you remember that little café we used to visit together in the rue de Sèvres? We were having an aperitif on the pavement one evening. It was *my* shoe then and the waiter kicked it flying. A number thirty-nine *autobus* ran over it and you had to buy me a new pair.'

Monsieur Pamplemousse felt his heart miss a beat. Shooting a set of *tricolores* still at red, he entered the Place des Ternes rather quicker than he had intended. Madame Pamplemousse hastily withdrew her hand as he fought to regain control of the car.

'I'm sorry, Aristide. That was my fault. I should not disturb you while you are driving.'

'That's all right, Couscous.' Monsieur Pamplemousse tried to keep the note of panic from his voice.

There was a stirring in the back seat. Ever alive to his master's moods, Pommes Frites was beginning to take an interest in things at long last, but for the time being it went unnoticed.

Even the most thick-skinned of animals would have sensed that all was not well, and Pommes Frites was no slouch when it came to following the drift of a conversation. It was an art he'd first acquired on his initial training course with the Paris police, and one which he'd managed to perfect during travels with his master when they'd been thrown into each other's company for many long hours at a time.

His vocabulary was small, depending on certain key words, but given those key words he was able to build up a fairly comprehensive and accurate picture of what was going on around him.

The key word in the present situation was undoubtedly 'shoe'. The word 'shoe' had definitely made him prick up his ears. It reminded him of the game he'd invented that evening; the ultimate rejection of which was yet another cause of his present mood.

It had been a good game while it lasted; one which had started out full of promise and which the other participants had given every sign of enjoying as well.

Like many an invention it wasn't entirely original—its human equivalent had many names, but basically it involved two players putting alternate hands one on top of the other as fast as they could while singing 'Pat-a-cake, pat-a-cake, baker's man . . .'

'Pommes Frites' was a simplified version for five players and took place under the table without the benefit of musical accompaniment. In the beginning it had consisted simply of his putting his paw down firmly on top of his master's shoe in order to relieve the boredom of what seemed like an interminable meal going on above his head. The results, however, had exceeded his wildest expectations; Monsieur Pamplemousse's foot responded with enthusiasm. Flushed with success, he'd tried putting his paw on other toes within range and in no time at all there were feet and shoes and legs everywhere. However, like all good things the game had eventually come to an end. Much to his disappointment, instead of the others following him out into the garden in hot pursuit of his master's shoe, as he had assumed they would, the front door slammed behind him and he found himself locked out.

Pommes Frites didn't normally suffer from pangs of remorse, still less from guilt complexes; the analyst's basket was not for him. However, looking back on things he couldn't help but feel that taking the shoe in the first place had been a mistake, burying it in a fit of pique a cardinal error. Somehow or other he felt responsible for his master's present mood and for the difficulties he was obviously encountering.

Adding it all up, putting two and two together, taking everything into account, all things considered, in Pommes Frites' humble opinion Monsieur Pamplemousse would be well advised to leave town as soon as possible, if not before, and with that thought uppermost in his mind he turned and faced the front, directing all his attention towards the back of his master's head.

Monsieur Pamplemousse, as it happened, was rapidly approaching a point where he would have needed very little encouragement to leave town.

No wonder the Director's wife had given him an odd look when they said their good-byes. Emboldened by the Armagnac and by what he'd taken to be her advances over dinner, he had prolonged his embrace rather more than he would normally have done, pressing into her hand at the very last moment a small *billet doux:* 'Your toes reveal what your eyes conceal.'

His heart sank as he remembered the words. He wondered if she would show it to the Director. She might even be reading it to him at that very moment. On the other hand, her response had not been entirely negative. A trifle cold at first, perhaps, but he'd put that down to the presence of her husband. There had been a more positive reaction at the very last moment. A kind of hesitating reappraisal of the situation, ending in a quick hug.

Either way it was not good news. It put an entirely different complexion on things.

'I'm not the only one who is being quiet, Aristide,' said Madame Pamplemousse as the lights of the Place de Clichy came into view. 'Are you worried about something?'

'Monsieur le Directeur has made me an offer.' Monsieur Pamplemousse made a snap decision as they turned a corner, crossed over the south-east tip of the Cimetière de Montmartre, and entered the relative gloom of the rue Caulaincourt. 'I may take him up on it. It will mean leaving tomorrow, but with my increment coming up . . .' He left the rest to Doucette's imagination.

Pommes Frites, settling down as best he could in the back of the car, heaved a sigh of relief.

'At least it will save us the problem of wondering whether we should ask them back or not.' Madame Pamplemousse sounded relieved too. The Director's house had been so grand, the thought of entertaining them was already beginning to bother her, especially with the kitchen still to be done. She was unsure where to place the Director. Their table was too small to put him all that far away.

Monsieur Pamplemousse read and understood her thoughts. It was a very feminine reaction. He took her left hand in his again. She gave it a quick squeeze.

'Will you be away for long?'

He shrugged. It was hard to say. In this instance there was no knowing. But it had always been that way. Working for *Le Guide* was no different in that respect from his days with the police. You set out on a project not knowing when you might return. On the other hand he liked it that way. So too, he suspected, did Doucette. It enabled her to 'get on with things.'

'I shall get on with things while you are away.'

'I'll send you a postcard.'

He always did. Usually a picture of the hotel where he was staying. There would be a cross marking his room. His whole life was contained between the covers of a postcard album.

'I'd better go out early and buy some things so that you can have a picnic.'

Pommes Frites pricked up his ears again. It was another of his 'key' words. Pommes Frites liked picnics. Before they arrived home he picked up one or two more; St. Georges-sur-Lie to name but a few. He wondered vaguely what it would be like there; if he would have to share his master's room or whether he would be allowed to sleep outside. Sleeping outside was nice and the nights were still warm.

He was still wondering next morning as Monsieur Pamplemousse packed the car ready for the journey. He was pleased to see his inflatable kennel being loaded into the boot. It was a good sign.

As they drove up the ramp and out of the garage, Monsieur Pamplemousse pushed his hand through the lift-up window and waved, in case Doucette was on the balcony to see them go.

The *boulangerie* on the corner was crowded; the butcher was arranging his window display. A black couple leaned out of a first floor window in the hotel opposite. A street cleaner on his *Caninette* was already out riding along the pavement looking for evidence of careless *chiens*. Pommes Frites gazed at him noncommittally.

Water gushed up out of the gutters and ran down the hill, guided on its way by the traditional mounds of rolled up carpet or sacking. Monsieur Pamplemousse followed its course as they headed towards *Le Guide*'s offices in the seventh arrondissement. By the sound of it they were likely to be away for a couple of weeks or more and there was some tidying up to do before he left. Besides, he must prepare a story for his colleagues, even though it went against the grain; even more so when he encountered sympathetic cluckings from the other early arrivals.

'Too bad.'

'Hope she's soon better.'

'Take care.'

A sleepy Operations Manager noted down the details and removed his flag from the map, putting it away in a drawer marked *'en suspens'*.

After he left the office, for no better reason than the fact that he encountered a traffic hold-up near the southern approaches to the *Périphérique*, Monsieur Pamplemousse doubled back down the rue Dantzig and immediately found himself caught up in a one-way system which took him further west than he had intended.

As he drove down the rue Dantzig he caught a glimpse of the *Ruche*, the old wine pavilion shaped like a bee-hive which had been left over from the 1900 Paris Exhibition and later turned into artists' studios. In its time it had housed Modigliani, Chagall and Léger, replacing the Bateau-Lavoir in Montmartre as a centre for inspiration. The sight of it caused him to make another snap decision, a minor change at the time, but one which was to have a profound effect on the days to come. Heading towards the *Périphérique* again, he turned right instead of left at the junction with the Boulevard Lefebvre.

The reason was simple. It was a nice day. The sun was shining. Why not take the pretty route out of Paris? He would go via Monet's old house at Giverny and picnic somewhere on the banks of the Seine. Perhaps near Nettle Island where Monet himself had loved to go. It would be a way of killing two birds with one stone. He'd been wanting to get on with an article he was preparing for *L'Escargot, Le Guide*'s staff magazine. It was on the subject of food in books and paintings, and like all such things it was taking longer than intended. There were diversions and side-tracks. For a start it had meant re-reading the whole of Zola with his descriptions of gargantuan meals born out of knowing what it was like to starve, living off sparrows in a Paris garret.

Truthfully, he was also in no great hurry to reach his destination. The more he thought about it in the cold light of day the less he liked the idea. It was a formidable task and he had a nasty feeling in the back of his mind that the Director hadn't come quite clean. Any diversion would be welcome if it put off the evil moment of his arrival.

Taking the Porte de Passy exit, they were soon in Bougival, whose soft light and river mists had been immortalised by Renoir and Manet and other painters over the years. Unlike Argenteuil, it still retained much of its old-world charm. He began to feel better. There were two good restaurants in Bougival. It was time they were reported on again. Perhaps, when he got back, he could entertain the Director and his wife there. It would be a way out of Doucette's problem.

Medan came and went. Medan, where Zola had lived and entertained before the Dreyfus case when he wrote *J'Accuse* and had to flee to England, ending up in a dreadful hotel where he wrote of biting on an unexpected clove in a cake. He wished he had a tenth of Zola's ability to recall tastes and smells. Not that it would have helped much in his work for *Le Guide* where everything, including smells, had to conform to a common standard, one person's writing indistinguishable from another's.

It was all very well the Director telling him he had to do something about improving the hotel. Hotels didn't improve overnight. There was more to it than that. It took time. Years of hard work. On the other hand, there must be *something* there; some spark which needed catching. Gault Millau seldom made mistakes, although clearly they had had second thoughts.

At Vernon he turned off for Giverny. They had made good time. The car park was nearly empty, the coaches had yet to arrive. The house with its walls made pink by grinding brick dust into the plaster was as he remembered it; the garden which in its heyday had kept six men at work was in full bloom.

He wandered down to the wistaria-clad Japanese bridge by the lily ponds, trying to picture the heavily bearded yet slightly dandyish figure of Monet, rising early in order to study the sunrise before embarking on one of his huge breakfasts of sausages and eggs, followed by toast and marmalade. Food, not art, would have been the subject under discussion. Monet loved good food, simple food he called it. *Asperges* from Argenteuil, truffles from Périgord, *cèpes* from his own cellar, brought up and cooked in the oven, wines from the Loire or from Burgundy, roast duck—its wings removed at the table and sent back for regrilling in a seasoning of pepper, salt and nutmeg as a special treat.

Elsie would have liked it. They would

have got on well together. She might even have coped with the old man in his more irascible moods, when things weren't going right and he made a bonfire of his work. She would probably have put her foot down over his monastic timetable. Lunch at eleven o'clock sharp; at this time of the year set out on a table beneath the linden trees. He looked at his own watch. It was barely eleven-thirty. Perhaps he would follow Monet's example and have an early lunch too. Already his taste buds were beginning to throb. The thought transmitted itself to Pommes Frites who wagged his tail in agreement.

A few minutes later they were on their way again, looking for a suitable spot.

Doucette had excelled herself with the picnic. Spiced beef, *pâté de campagne*, smoked cod's roe, chicken and ham pie, salad in a separate container, a crisp *ficelle*, sorbet in a freezing jar, *tarte aux pommes, fromage*, a bottle of Pommard and another of Badoit. The small picnic table he always carried in the boot was soon filled; the tablecloth hidden beneath all the goodies. A sunshade in position, Monsieur Pamplemousse unclipped one of the car seats, put it carefully into place, removed his tie, tucked a large serviette into the top of his shirt, and took a firm grasp of his knife and fork as he prepared to do battle.

Perhaps he should play *pieds* under the table more often. It was very rare he was given such a treat. There was even a bone for Pommes Frites. The thought crossed his mind that perhaps Doucette wanted him out of the way; maybe she had taken the Director's advances seriously. He dismissed the idea. Much more likely she had a guilty conscience. Besides, the Director had Elsie to contend with.

He wondered if the Director's wife would answer his note. Luckily Doucette never opened his mail. All the same, the thought made him feel hot under the collar.

Mopping his brow with the serviette, he helped himself to some more pie, cutting off an equal portion for Pommes Frites. It disappeared before his own was halfway to his mouth.

The Seine had a purplish sheen to it in the September sunshine; the Pommard was a real treat. A single vineyard. He made a mental note to call in the next time he was down that way and replenish his stocks. It would make a nice diversion.

The thought triggered off another. Why

not call in and see Bernard on the way to St. Georges-sur-Lie? Helping himself to a wedge of *Saint-Paulin*, he went to the car for his map. Mortagne-au-Perche wouldn't be too far out of his way. *En route* to Bernard he could stop off at a garden centre and buy him a rose. Perhaps a 'Maiden's Blush'. He would appreciate the joke.

Afterwards he could go via Illiers-Combray where Marcel Proust had spent childhood holidays with his Tante Léonie, dipping spoonfuls of madeleine crumbs into her lime tea.

As he cleared away the picnic things, Monsieur Pamplemousse tried to recall the exact details of Bernard's case. He'd been away in Alsace at the time and so had missed out on all the juicy bits. By the time he got back to the office there were other things to talk about.

What was it the Director had said? Remember Bernard. Don't let it happen to you. Don't let *what* happen? Once again, he had a nasty feeling the Director was being less than frank. There were areas of a decided greyness.

It took a while to find Bernard's house. Mortagne, high up above the surrounding countryside, was busily provincial. He stopped in the main street to ask the way. The first two people professed not to know; the third was so bubbling over with excitement, mistaking him for a journalist, he had a job to get away and through-traffic behind ground to a halt, hooting impatiently.

As the Director had surmised, Bernard was tending his roses, dead-heading a bed of *Gloire de Dijon,* looking for outward-facing buds like a man with time on his hands.

'Coaches used to stop and admire these,' he said gloomily, after they had exchanged greetings. 'They still come, but mostly to stare at me.'

Monsieur Pamplemousse opened the boot of his car and produced his gift. He rather regretted his choice now. Bernard seemed to have taken things hard. He decided not to make too much of it.

'I'm not sure of the name. It is pink with white towards the edges. It dates back to before 1738. The man at the nursery said it should grow well.'

Bernard brightened. 'You know, it's kind of you to call. I often think of you. In a way our two cases are very much alike. I mean, the way you were found hanging about in the toilets at the Follies without any clothes.'

'I was not hanging about,' said Monsieur Pamplemousse stiffly. 'I was merely taking refuge. I had no clothes because they had been taken from me at gun point. The whole thing was a frame-up. A plot to discredit me.'

'I really meant that in the end it was your word against theirs,' Bernard broke in defensively. 'If I remember rightly they never did find your assailant.' He led the way towards the house and pointed to a table and some chairs set out under a tree. 'Make yourself comfortable. I'll fetch something to drink.'

He reappeared a moment later carrying a tray. Monsieur Pamplemousse watched while he poured out a Kir. The Cassis bore the Chapel label. Bernard must have bought it on his travels. He'd had it once before, home-made, rich and fruity, made to the highest standards. He felt honoured at being given such a treat. The wine was a Sancerre; the bottle glistening with beads of cold on its outside.

'What happened?' he asked, trying to jog the other's memory before the conversation took a turn. 'I was away at the time.'

Bernard gazed gloomily at his glass and then took a copious draught. 'I still don't

49

really know. I mean I don't know what came over me. It was during that hot spell we had earlier in the year. That didn't help. I'd had a large lunch. That didn't help either. I started to feel rather strange soon after I set off and after I'd driven about sixty or seventy kilometres it got so that I could hardly stand it.'

'What sort of strange?'

'Well, that's just it. Nothing like it has ever happened to me before . . . at least, not in the same way. I mean . . . sort of . . .'

Monsieur Pamplemousse watched in surprise as Bernard started shrugging his shoulders and winking, whilst at the same time emitting a series of shrill whistling noises.

'You mean . . . you felt like *une coucherie?* A little diversion?'

Bernard blushed. 'You can say that again. I tell you, I don't usually go in for that sort of thing, but if *une fille de plaisir* had come along at that moment I don't know what I would have done. Well, I do . . . I was beginning to feel quite desperate. More than that . . .'

'More?' Monsieur Pamplemousse raised his eyebrows enquiringly.

50

Bernard blushed again and then mopped his brow. He poured out another Kir. 'I felt as though I could have taken on all comers, if you'll pardon the expression. I felt like the prize stallion at the Cadre Noir. Unfortunately, I was miles from anywhere. At least, I thought I was miles from anywhere.'

Monsieur Pamplemousse found himself hoping Bernard had a good lawyer. If he found himself in the dock up against a prosecuting counsel who meant business he wouldn't stand a chance.

'So what happened then?'

'I parked by the side of the road and went into a wood meaning to try and sleep it off. I'd put it down to too much drink. I was in such a state by then I sort of—well, it sounds a bit silly talking about it across a table like this—but I got lost. I must have been going round and round in circles. That was when I heard all these voices.'

'Voices?' Monsieur Pamplemousse reached for the bottle. His throat felt unaccountably dry. 'What sort of voices?'

'Girls' voices. I'd parked near a school. A convent, actually, which makes it sound even worse. You know what convent girls are supposed to be like. They were on some

51

sort of ramble. I bumped into them in a clearing and . . .'

'And?'

'They say I started behaving in a funny kind of way. Like . . . beckoning to them . . .'

'Beckoning?'

Bernard nodded. 'I can actually remember doing it in a hazy sort of way. First of all some big blonde sixth-former came over.' He paused in order to emit another series of whistles. 'I think she must have been in charge. Then the others followed.'

'Beckoning doesn't sound a very major crime,' said Monsieur Pamplemousse thoughtfully. 'I don't see what all the fuss is about. A good lawyer . . .'

'It depends,' said Bernard, slowly and carefully, 'on what you beckon with. What's annoying is that I'm sure most of them weren't really bothered. They seemed to be enjoying it—the big blonde one especially —she started to undo her blouse. Then one of the juniors began to cry. Now they've all ganged up on me. It's thirty against one— I don't stand a chance. Besides, one of them had a camera. Blown up and in colour it won't look good in court. The Mother Superior definitely has it in for me.'

Monsieur Pamplemousse stayed to finish the bottle of wine and then at a suitable moment took his leave. The visit had done little to raise his spirits; rather the reverse. As he drove off Bernard was busy removing his new rose from its container. From all he'd said he would have plenty of time to nurture it during the coming months. No wonder the Director had talked about having to pull strings.

At Illiers-Combray he stopped as a matter of course at 4 rue du Docteur-Proust. Like Monet, Proust had enjoyed what might be called 'simple food'. *Sole meunière* had been one of his favourites. Scrambled eggs another. He wondered if he had followed Escoffier's advice and speared a clove of garlic with the fork before making them.

On the door there was a sign: 'Hours open 14.15–17.00. Next tour 16.00'. He looked at his watch. Just too late.

In the square opposite the church with its forbidding interior, there was a shop selling madeleines, shell-shaped as they always had been after the shells pilgrims to Santiago-de-Compostela had worn in their hats. He toyed with the idea of buying some, but his mind was on other things. It was like starting off a case in the old days. He needed to put himself in the right mood. Sometimes that took days, during which time he knew he wasn't always good to live with.

Pommes Frites, dozing off his lunch in the car, opened one eye sleepily as Monsieur Pamplemousse climbed back in.

Abandoning all thoughts of his article for the time being, Monsieur Pamplemousse put his foot down hard for the rest of the journey. The article could wait. Proust had died in 1922, Monet in 1926—two years before he himself had been born. Zola in 1902. His current problem was of the present and suddenly he was anxious to get to grips with it. If he arrived at St. Georges-sur-Lie in good time he would be able to take Pommes Frites for a pre-dinner stroll round the village so that they could get the feel of it.

After Illiers he drove through kilometre after kilometre of open hedgeless farmland between flower-decorated villages with only the occasional black-faced sheep—the Bleu de Maine of the area—to watch him pass. The very monotony gave him time to think. No wonder the area had a high suicide rate. The warning bells were growing louder; more to do with things that hadn't been said rather than those which had. Gradually the scenery became more wooded again. Here and there a thatched cottage dotted the land-scape and the road wound past half-hidden *boires*—hollow dried-up areas the Loire would flood later in the year.

St. Georges was on him almost before he realised it. First a farm building with a faded Dubonnet advertisement painted on the side, then another with an equally faded sign: 'Hôtel du Paradis 200m.'

As he turned into a square he found him-self facing the hotel itself. Stone steps, grey and time-worn, led up to an oak door open to the street. At first floor level there was a long balcony. To the right there was a small garden with climbing roses against the wall and a few tables and chairs set out under a yew tree; doubtless in its time it had watched over many a wedding party or christening celebration. Nailed to its trunk was a notice: PARKING. Below it an arrow pointed towards the back of the hotel.

Driving through the square he spotted one of the new automatic Sanisettes which were already commonplace in Paris. It had been placed not far from the hotel dining-room, its entrance door discreetly facing the other way. Not discreetly enough appar-ently, for someone had already sprayed the word NON in large black letters on the outside.

Reflecting that the invention of the aerosol was a mixed blessing, he looked around. Peace reigned supreme. There was hardly a soul about. Window boxes filled with begonias and periwinkles adorned the window ledges of houses to his left, geraniums and nasturtiums overflowed on to the cobblestones. To the right there was a sprinkling of shops; a *boucherie*, a *droguerie*—its brooms and plastic bowls spilling out over the narrow pavement, a *bureau de tabac* and a small *pharmacie*, all dozing in the afternoon sun.

In a side street leading down to the right of the hotel there was a grocery store and next to that on a corner, the *boulangerie;* beyond that a cluster of farm buildings and a line of weeping willows showing where the river must be, then open country again.

As he turned into the hotel car park he felt rather than saw a movement in the far corner near a row of stables, as if someone had dodged out of sight.

There was one other car; a Renault 14 with a 75 Paris number plate. As he drew up behind it he noticed its windows were covered in steam. Either someone was boiling a kettle inside, which seemed unlikely, or else . . . even as the thought entered his mind a hand reached up and rubbed a patch clear on the back window. A moment later a woman's head appeared in the hole. Her face was flushed, her hair awry, her lipstick smudged. She looked as though she had been pulled through a hedge backwards, pulled through for a reason which was not hard to fathom.

She looked somewhat taken aback as she focused her gaze on to Monsieur Pamplemousse not more than a couple of metres away; even more so when she caught sight of Pommes Frites staring unblinkingly from the passenger seat.

Monsieur Pamplemousse raised his hat and then backed politely away, parking as far as he could from the other car. His mind was racing. Once again the Director's parting words came back to him, only this time more clearly. Something clicked in his mind. The warning bells were now much louder.

Signalling Pommes Frites to follow him he made his way out of the car park towards a telephone kiosk he'd noticed on a corner near the square. As they passed a lane at the side of the *boulangerie* he saw the doors were open; no doubt to let the heat from the ovens out. A blue Renault van was parked nearby. He nodded to a bearded man in white overalls who was watching him from the doorway, but it wasn't acknowledged. Instead the man turned and went inside.

He dialled his office number. 'Véronique . . . Pamplemousse here. Give me Monsieur le Directeur, please.'

There was a pause. A long pause. He got ready for the encounter to come.

'I'm sorry, Monsieur Pamplemousse. Monsieur le Directeur says to tell you he left early.' The voice at the other end sounded aggrieved on his behalf. It was the voice of one who did not take kindly to repeating so palpable a falsehood to someone she knew. He decided not to make an issue of it and compound her embarrassment.

'Never mind. Do you have Bernard's telephone number?'

There was another pause. Shorter this time. 'He has changed his number. It is now ex-directory.'

'It is most important.'

'Do you have a pencil?'

He wrote it down and murmured his thanks.

'How is your aunt, Monsieur Pamplemousse?'

'It is hard to say at this moment in time. I am reserving judgment.'

'If there is anything else I can do for you . . .' He repeated his thanks and then hung up.

Bernard sounded slightly out of breath. Doubtless he was still in the garden.

'I will not keep you. I have just one question to ask. It is to do with your misfortune. Tell me where you had lunch that day.'

The reply confirmed his worst suspicions. The meal he'd eaten in St. Georges-sur-Lie had obviously left a deep impression on Bernard.

'It was one of the worst I can remember. A little place not far from Saumur. The chief asked me to call in there, God knows why . . .'

Monsieur Pamplemousse allowed the voice to drone on, but his mind was hardly on the conversation as he stared out at the toilet on the other side of the square. For two pins, if he'd had an aerosol he would have added the Director's name to its concrete façade. How could anyone be so two-faced, so . . . so . . . Words failed him.

'Thank you, Bernard . . . you too . . .'

He paused as a thought struck him. 'Take care—and Bernard, I cannot promise, but if it is at all possible, if all goes well, you understand—I may be able to help you with your problem. I will be in touch. *Au revoir*. I must go now. I have another call to make.'

He stood for a moment lost in thought, then he picked up the phone and inserted another coin in the box.

'It's me again . . . Pamplemousse. There *is* something else you can do for me. Several things, in fact.'

If Véronique was surprised to hear his voice again she didn't register it; his list of requirements drew no comment.

'I will do my best, Monsieur Pample-mousse.'

'Can you address them to me care of *Poste Restante*, Tours, and mark them urgent.'

'*Oui*, Monsieur Pamplemousse.'

'When I get back, Véronique, I will give you a large tin of *rillettes*. It will, if I have my way, be made not from the pigs of Angers, but from Monsieur le Directeur's own flesh and bones.'

Replacing the receiver before the other

had time to reply, he came out into the sunshine again and gazed up at the Hôtel du Paradis.

Still waters indeed! Deep, dark, muddy, blacker than black waters more like it; waters thick with mire. No wonder Michelin hadn't seen fit to award the hotel a red rocking chair; by the sound of it a red mattress would have been more to the point.

Pommes Frites followed the direction of his master's gaze, taking in the ivy covered walls and the dining-room to the left of the entrance, its tables already set for dinner. He knew a good hotel when he saw one. There would be steaks; rich, succulent steaks, red and oozing with juice; liver, and bones—lots of fresh, juicy bones to gnaw. He couldn't wait to get at them.

Together they made their way towards the front door, each busy with his own thoughts. Their steps reflected their moods. Pommes Frites' were jaunty and full of anticipation. Monsieur Pamplemousse's, on the other hand, were grim and purposeful; they were the steps of a man with a mission; a man who might not as yet know quite where that mission would take him but, come what may, no one was going to stop him completing it. The saving of Bernard

61

was rapidly taking precedence over the saving of the Hôtel du Paradis.

—— 3 ——————————————————

Dinner for Two

BREATHING HEAVILY AFTER his exertions with a towel, Monsieur Pamplemousse paused and gazed disbelievingly at a *bidet* which stood below and slightly forward of the washbasin in his bathroom. A mirror above the basin reflected Pommes Frites peering round the open door leading to the bedroom. He, too, was registering disbelief. Disbelief tinged with growing concern was written large all over his face as he watched his master slide the *bidet* out on its rails and remove, one by one, and in the reverse order in which they had been carefully placed ready for dinner, underpants, a shirt, trousers and a bedraggled pair of socks. Pommes Frites did not wag his tail. He sensed it was not a tail-wagging occasion.

Also reflected in the glass was the mirror image of the obligatory card on the back of the bathroom door giving the number of the room and the price, *par nuit, par personne,* together with a list of the various facilities it included. In this case the *chambre* was *numéro un,* and apart from a *grand lit* and a *balcon,* it included a *salle de bains* containing a *bain,* a *lavabo* and a *bidet.* *Petit déjeuner* was twenty francs extra; *chiens* fifteen.

The Hôtel du Paradis boasted four other bedrooms offering between them a choice of *lavabo* and *bidet, douche* and *lavabo, W.C.* and *bidet,* or just a *douche* and *bidet.* But in none of them was it possible to enjoy all five facilities at the same time.

In the end, so great had been his desire for a long and relaxing bath after the journey, Monsieur Pamplemousse had chosen *numero un,* above the dining-room and facing the square. It had seemed well worth the extra twenty francs a night and if the worst came to the worst he could always make use of the automatic toilet in the square outside. Now he was beginning to regret his choice.

Not only was the room, with its hideously unforgettable flowered wallpaper, one of the most depressingly uncomfortable he had encountered in a long time, filled with dust-ridden sporting trophies and furnished with bizarre examples of bygone carpentry handed down from another era, the plumbing in the *salle de bains* had to be seen to be believed.

Undecided-looking pipes emerged from the unlikeliest of places and hovered before setting off in various unexpected directions. Some were sawn-off and plugged; others disappeared into yet more holes in the wall never to reappear again. The one thing they all had in common was the fact that they had been installed by someone possessed of an unswerving belief in the adage that the shortest distance between two points was a straight line; which gave rise to an effect not unlike that of the engine-room of an early submarine; cramped and dangerous. Taking a bath had not been an enjoyable experience. The only saving grace was a heater in the middle of the wall. Operated by a cord switch, it had been installed with a blind disregard for the laws of safety, probably by the same hand responsible for the plumbing, but its warm glow offered a welcome contrast to the rapidly cooling water which emerged from the tap marked CHAUD.

All of which wouldn't have been so bad, but when he went to clean his teeth in the washbasin, scalding hot water from an entirely different system gushed forth from a tap marked FROID and made his bristles go soggy with surprise.

But the unkindest cut of all happened when he emptied the basin and discovered that for some strange reason the waste pipe went via the *bidet*. The one bright spot was that he hadn't been sitting on it at the time. Getting his clothes wet was bad enough, but clothes could be dried and ironed. He shuddered to think of the suffering that might have been caused to his bare and sensitive flesh had it been in the path of the same water that had practically melted the handle of his toothbrush.

What particularly grieved him was the fact that the trousers were his special working ones; the pair with a secret compartment in the right leg—a modification of Madame Pamplemousse's which enabled him to conceal his notebook beneath the folds of a table-cloth while making out his reports. Thankfully the notebook itself was still on the bed where he'd left it. He had a feeling he would be making good use of it before his stay was out.

Dressed once again in the clothes he'd worn for the journey, he crossed and opened the French windows leading to the balcony. The square was deserted; the few shops closed for the day. Below him and a little to one side stood the Sanisette. Its concrete façade looked slightly out of place alongside the other buildings, but no doubt in time it would become an accepted part of the scene.

Through a gap in the houses on the far side of the square he could see fields of *asperges*, through another gap some goats. Beyond that fields of fading sunflowers rose majestically towards the clear September sky, their huge yellow heads bowed down under the weight of it all. The sight reminded him that he had work to do. Apart from their health-giving properties, sunflower seeds were thought by some to have aphrodisiac powers, probably on account of the impression they gave of drinking in the sun's rays; an association of ideas. Perhaps . . . perhaps even now someone in the village was stirring a cauldron ready for the evening meal.

Almost immediately he dismissed the idea. Deep down he had a feeling that the cause of Bernard's fall from grace would be nothing quite as obvious; an accident rather than a deliberate act. His meeting with the Director's aunt had been necessarily brief —a quick exchange of pleasantries while he'd been checking in, but his first impression had been of someone almost transparently honest, and he believed in first impressions. Instinct told him that whatever had happened to Bernard was not of her making.

Turning back into the room he nearly tripped over Pommes Frites who lay with his chin between his paws gazing lugubriously at the head of a lion-skin rug on the floor at the foot of the bed. There must at one time have been a taxidermist of note in the area. In Tours several years before he'd come across a stuffed elephant which had belonged to Barnum and Bailey's circus, and in the same city he'd once stayed at an hotel where there was a stuffed lion standing in a make-believe jungle by the lift shaft. He'd even come across the odd stuffed horse standing around in fields during his travels.

Whoever it was had been kept well supplied by Tante Louise's forebears. Animals or heads of animals stood or peered down from walls on all sides as they left the room, silently following their progress as they made their way down the stairs.

An air of gloom enveloped them as they descended to the ground floor. Monsieur Pamplemousse was not a devotee of the art of the taxidermist. On the whole stuffed animals made him feel depressed. It was a feeling that was clearly endorsed by Pommes Frites, who glanced uneasily at a large brown bear who stood expectantly holding a tray marked POSTE behind the reception desk. Pommes Frites liked other creatures to react. You knew where you were with creatures that reacted.

Monsieur Pamplemousse's spirits sank still further as they entered the dining-room. There were about twenty tables; some seventy places in all, but only one was occupied, and that by a young couple who looked as if they were there for the peace and quiet rather than the food.

He looked around and was about to take his seat near the window and as far away from the others as possible, when the door leading to the kitchen swung open.

'Vous avez une réservation'? The voice went with its owner, a large, well-preserved madame of uncertain age who bustled forward clutching a menu with the air of one used to being in command. Monsieur Pamplemousse had met her counterpart a thousand times before, in bars, bistros and tiny restaurants the length and breadth of France. She would be a widow, married once to a man who had died in a war. What-

ever the time they were always of a previous age, just as they had been in Napoleon's time. *Formidable* was the only word to describe them.

'No, Madame,' he began. 'I—'

'In that case, Monsieur . . .' Her words were punctuated by a thud as a plastic RÉSERVÉE notice was grasped and plonked down very firmly in the centre of the table by a hand which continued on its way in one sweeping movement towards another table near the couple in the corner.

Monsieur Pamplemousse braced himself. If it was to be a battle of wills then it was one which needed to be won early on in his stay rather than later. He had no wish to be seated next to the only other occupants of an otherwise empty room, simply to save someone else's feet.

He pointed in turn to a compromise position on the other side of the window. 'I would prefer that one.'

The pause was only fractional; the flicker in the eyes that met and held his was one of respect rather than disapproval. As was so often the case, challenge was the best form of defence.

Pommes Frites, confident of the outcome of the argument, brought it to a conclusion by settling himself under the table, awaiting his master's choice. He hoped it would be something he could get his teeth into. Something meaty. A large steak, perhaps—or some *carré d'agneau*. Something that would allow for a reasonable division. Experience told him he would not have to put up with any newfangled cooking—all slivers of underdone meat with bits of fruit on top and brightly coloured vegetables. Pommes Frites was not a devotee of *nouvelle cuisine*.

Experience told Monsieur Pamplemousse as he ran his eye down the *carte* that neither of them was in for a gastronomic treat. It was handwritten in purple ink—often a good sign, but in this case in letters so faded they had obviously been penned many months before. He looked in vain for an additional list of dishes of the day. No piece of paper fell out from between the pages when he held up the folder and shook it. There wasn't even a dish that the chef—or, as he suspected, the Director's aunt, had marked with an asterisk as being particularly recommended; a speciality of the house.

He glanced around the room at the empty tables, each with its quota of napkins folded hog's-head style on top of the waiting plates, surrounded by sets of rather sad-looking cutlery. The enormity of the task in front of him suddenly sank home. On the one hand there was his brief to put forward or even to implement suggestions as to how to bring about improvements in the restaurant. On the other hand there was the problem of discovering what dish or combination of dishes had caused Bernard to disgrace himself after his visit.

He ran his eye down the menu, considering the options. There were many foods credited with the power to increase sexual desires, most of them he'd covered in an article for *L'Escargot*. Others promoted 'staying power'. He'd once read that in India men rubbed garlic ointment on their vital parts in moments of need. A sobering thought which momentarily put him off the *potage aioli*. Besides, Bernard's 'staying power' under what might be called 'field conditions' had hardly been put to the test. Perhaps it was something he had drunk? Perhaps some brandy, egg-yolk and cinnamon concoction had triggered it off? Again, that would have been a deliberate act totally out of character with the Bernard he knew. Looking at the row of bottles behind a small bar near the entrance to the dining-room he could see a selection of various marques of cognac and a sprinkling of Armagnacs, but there wasn't even a bottle of advocaat and he doubted very much if the hotel was into serving any kind of 'concoction'. It would be a bottle of cognac plonked on the table along with a glass and a 'help yourself'. The request for an egg to go with it would have been greeted by a sniff. He shuddered to think what would happen if you asked for cinnamon as well.

Tia Maria was supposed to heat the blood, but that, too, was absent and it would have needed a great many glasses to induce in Bernard the kind of blood heat that would have caused him to behave as he had.

On the other hand, perhaps unwittingly he'd stumbled on a selection of dishes which against all the odds had combined to produce an unprecedented effect; like someone discovering a system to beat the bank at Monte Carlo. He resolved to put his theory to the test. There was no time like the present and he was hardly likely to lose control of his emotions with the waitress.

Moules were nowhere on the *carte*, fish with ginger was obviously an unheard of concept, frogs' legs were conspicuous by their absence.

In the end mentally, and without any great feeling of optimism, he settled on artichoke—once sold in the streets of Paris because of its 'heating qualities', cow's liver—something the Romans had set great faith in, drying it in order to grind up as part of a love potion—and *tourte au lapin* with spinach and potato. With luck, being in the Loire Valley the pie would be made with prunes as well. Prunes figured largely in local recipes, and in the old days they had been served in brothels to stimulate the customers and promote a brisk turn around in the trade. As for potato; no less an authority than William Shakespeare had pointed out its aphrodisiac qualities in *The Merry Wives of Windsor*. If none of that had any effect he might end up with *ananas; ananas* with sugar piled high on top, followed by an Armagnac.

Feeling pleased that his research had borne fruit, Monsieur Pamplemousse sat back and wondered what Bernard's choice had been. Had it been the forty franc menu with the rabbit pie, or the forty-five one with liver? Perhaps he had done as he was now doing, gone the whole hog and eaten *à la carte*. He wished now he'd thought to telephone and ask, but it was too late; the

Madame was already advancing towards him at a brisk pace, pencil and pad poised for action. With only two other customers and the prospect of an early night she would not take kindly to any delay.

'*Vous avez choisi Monsieur*'? She flicked open the pad.

His choice went without comment until he asked for *pommes frites* with the *lapin*.

'*Non, Monsieur.*'

'*Non?*'

'*Non. Pommes vapeur.*' Again their eyes met. Again there was a feeling of a battle to be fought. He wondered whether *frites* were not available—too much trouble, or whether his choice had simply met with disapproval. Hearing his name mentioned, Pommes Frites poked his head out enquiringly. For the sake of peace Monsieur Pamplemousse decided on a tactical withdrawal.

He nodded his agreement. '*Pommes vapeur.*' She was probably right. Gastronomically speaking it was a better combination. *Frites* would soak up the rich juices from the pie and lose their crispness. It had really been a concession to a 'certain other' not a million miles away. Pommes Frites was not keen on *vapeur*, he liked his namesake best, often eating large quantities.

Looking rather put-out, he disappeared under the table again.

His capitulation was rewarded by a slight thawing out. 'I would not recommend the *pommes frites*, Monsieur.' It was said with feeling born of past experience. '*Terminé?*' Without waiting for a reply, the *carte de table* was exchanged for a basket of bread and the *carte des vins*.

Monsieur Pamplemousse gazed at both with an equal lack of enthusiasm. The bread looked like a poor imitation of the Poilâne wheat loaves presently fashionable in Paris. Long-lasting and delicious when baked by Poilâne, but from the tired look of the slices he'd been given they must have long ago outlived their life expectancy. Why, in heaven's name, did they serve it when there was a perfectly good *boulangerie* not a stone's throw away?

He opened the *carte des vins* and as he did so his spirits rose slightly. Not unexpectedly, it was the usual commercially available booklet, sectionalised and decorated with anonymous men operating ancient presses. The pages had been inscribed by someone using the same purple ink as had been used for the *carte de table*. What was surprising was the fact that although none of the entries

75

had been accorded a vintage there were some very familiar names; mouth-watering names. The Bordeaux section in particular sported some highly respected representatives of the 1855 classification.

He hesitated, trying to decide whether to choose a local wine as he'd intended or something more exotic. Again, he found himself wondering about Bernard. Had he opted for a half carafe of the house wine, included in the price of the menu, or had he indulged himself? If the Kir they'd had that afternoon was anything to go by, he suspected the latter.

His choice of a Ducru Beaucaillou met with a total lack of response. The bottle when it arrived was covered in dust. He reached forward and felt it quickly while the waitress searched under her apron for a corkscrew. It was cold from the cellar. Catching her eye he withdrew his hand again, waiting while she opened it. He half expected her to pass the cork under her nose and then pour it without comment, but in the event he detected a hint of grudging approval in her perfunctory sniff.

Swirling the wine round in the glass he looked at it against the white cloth. The colour was surprisingly rich. It was rich to the nose as well, with a cedary bouquet. It had a feeling of depth and age which over-rode the coldness to the lips. He decided to take his meal at as leisurely a pace as possible so that it would have time to open up.

As he put the glass down again he caught sight of the year on the label. It was a '66. He could hardly believe his good fortune.

'This is the wine which is on the list?'

The waitress craned her neck, taking in both the list and the label. '*Oui*. There is something wrong?'

Monsieur Pamplemousse made a non-committal gesture. He had done his duty. If the hotel wished to offer wine at give-away prices that was their business. He had no wish to query his good fortune any more for fear it would go away.

'*Terminé?*' As the wine list disappeared from under his nose in a manner which brooked no further argument he resolved to make a closer study of it at the earliest op-portunity. Who knew what other goodies were contained within its pages? Left on his own again he held the cork below the folds of the table cloth. An approving sniff greeted its appearance. Pommes Frites liked red Bordeaux. It always gave him an appetite. Sometimes he was allowed the dregs in his water bowl. He especially liked the crunchy bits. In his opinion the more crunchy bits there were the better the wine.

As if to underline the change in their fortunes, the setting sun, which had been half-hidden behind a building, cast a shaft of evening brightness across the table. It carried on across the room, illuminating the flushed faces of the couple in the corner. There was a flurry of movement and for a moment or two Monsieur Pamplemousse gazed at them, wondering if perhaps they were falling victims to Bernard's disease. He decided not. It was merely young love. All the same, it might be worth keeping an eye on their choice of food.

Throwing caution to the wind, he withdrew his notebook from a side pocket and began to write, slowly and methodically awarding points here, taking away others there, totting up the pluses and the minuses since their arrival.

Looked at from any direction his deliberations made sorry reading. Mathematically it could have been reduced to a series of figures which grew less and less equal the more the meal progressed.

The arrival of the rabbit pie reminded

him of the Director's words. 'Pastry, Pamplemousse, that would tax the ingenuity of a woodpecker.' If the noise coming from under the table was anything to go by, even Pommes Frites was having trouble masticating it. He reached down and gave him an encouraging pat. He wished now he'd insisted on *frites* after all. The rich juices he'd pictured savouring were non-existent. It was a meal of unbelievable awfulness. Had there been less at stake he would have sent a message to the kitchen congratulating the Director's aunt on her effrontery. Several times during the course of the evening Pommes Frites looked out from under the table-cloth as if he could hardly believe his eyes let alone his taste buds.

Halfway through the sweet course Monsieur Pamplemousse reached for his tablets. Dyspepsia was an occupational hazard and although he was blessed with a moderately good digestive system, there were limits to its powers of endurance. He slipped a second one under the table. Pommes Frites crunched it gratefully.

'*Terminé?*'

'*Oui.*' There was nothing more to be said. He contemplated Madame Terminé through half-closed eyes, wondering if his meal had brought about any great change. Sadly it had not. It was possible that beneath her tightly corsetted exterior there beat a heart of gold, but if so neither food nor wine had made it any easier to detect. She flicked the table with her napkin.

'*Café?*'

'*Non.*' Coffee after such a meal might only compound the problem of going to sleep. 'Do you have a *tisane*'?

'Here or in the *salon?*' The emphasis on the last word was such that any suggestion of a choice was clearly window-dressing. He wondered what the reaction would be if he insisted on taking it at his table. Not wishing to be relegated to the cheerless room he'd seen on first entering the hotel, he decided on another approach.

'I'll take it up to my room.'

As they left the dining-room the young couple in the corner were already receiving their marching orders in the form of a folded bill on a plate. The restaurant of the Hôtel du Paradis was definitely being terminéed for the night.

On the way to the stairs he hesitated, torn between going straight up to his room or going out of the back entrance to the hotel in order to inflate Pommes Frites' kennel for the night. He had just decided in favour of carrying on up the stairs—the kennel could wait until they took their post-prandial stroll—when he caught sight of the Director's aunt through an open doorway at the end of the passage. Dressed in a long white apron, she looked rather more tired and fraught than he remembered from his arrival earlier in the evening.

Partly on an impulse and partly out of curiosity he made his way towards the kitchen. Almost immediately he regretted the decision. His appearance prompted the inevitable question which he should have foreseen.

'Did I enjoy my meal?' He played for time before answering. Natural politeness towards a member of the opposite sex suggested a non-committal answer. His training with *Le Guide* forbade anything other than a non-committal answer. But his taste buds and his digestive juices, not to mention his reason for being there told him it was necessary to be cruel in order to be kind.

'With the greatest respect, and since you have asked, I cannot remember when I had a worse meal!'

Her jaw dropped and for a moment he thought she was going to cry.

'I'm sorry to put it quite so bluntly, but I would not be doing you a favour if I did otherwise. The artichoke was under-cooked—I had to tug the leaves away from the heart. It was also discoloured. If you are going to prepare it days ahead then it should have had a slice of lemon tied to it to prevent that happening. And it is not sufficient just to put it on a plate; it should have been served with melted butter or with hollan-daise.

'As for the *lapin*—dying of old age is one thing, encasing it within pastry so hard it could have served as a funeral casket is an-other matter again. And when you keep *pommes vapeur* hot you should cover them with a cloth. In that way you will absorb any excess moisture and they will arrive at the table dry and floury instead of sodden as the ones were tonight.

'Even the pineapple had not been treated with respect. Clearly it had spent over-long in a refrigerator—upright at that. It should have been kept at room temperature on its side in a paper bag and turned regularly. Keep a pineapple upright and all the flavour disappears. Also it should be cut down-wards with the grain—not across.'

Madame Louise gazed at him curiously

as she digested the information. 'You speak knowledgeably,' she ventured at last. 'Justine told me you were making notes over your meal. Are you in the same business?'

Realising that in giving vent to his indignation he might have gone too far, Monsieur Pamplemousse interrupted her hastily.

'I am interested, that is all. I was making notes for a book I am writing. It is set here, in the Loire Valley. Your Madame Terminé would do better if she attended to the needs of your customers rather than their actions—which are none of her business.'

Turning to remove a kettle from the stove, Madame Louise gave a laugh. It transformed her features. Monsieur Pamplemousse felt his bad temper evaporate. As it did so there came a sudden feeling of guilt and a desire to help. She reached up for a tin. 'Justine would not be pleased if she heard you call her that.'

'It is true,' said Monsieur Pamplemousse defensively. 'She would be more at home in a station buffet making sure everyone caught the last train.'

The Director's aunt gave a wry smile as she added water to the cup. 'All the same, I do not know what I would do without her. Doing the cooking is bad enough. Finding the food to fit the menu is worse. Sometimes I have to go as far as Tours.'

'If you'll forgive my saying so,' broke in Monsieur Pamplemousse, 'that is quite the wrong way to go about things. You should always make the menu fit the food.' How many times had he heard chefs utter those very words? You went to the market early and bought well, then you returned and wrote the menu around the food.

'If you buy the best of ingredients you can never really fail. It is more than half the battle. You may end up with something you hadn't intended, but it won't be an out and out disaster.'

Well, hardly ever, he added under his breath. There were always exceptions to every rule.

Brushing a strand of hair from her eyes, Madame Louise looked up at him. 'That is a man talking. Men are always so full of confidence. It is hard for a woman when she is on her own with no one to turn to.'

As he took the tray from her Monsieur Pamplemousse was reminded once again of the Director's words.

'I understand. I'm sorry if I sounded a little abrupt just now, but you did ask.'

'You were quite right to tell me. Perhaps

if more people did that, life would be easier. Do you have any more complaints?'

'Since you ask, there is a little matter of the plumbing in my room. There appears to be a problem with the waste pipe from the hand basin. It connects with the *bidet*. I'm afraid I had an accident earlier this evening. If you have an iron I could borrow I would be grateful.'

As he made his way up the stairs Monsieur Pamplemousse felt himself being watched. Glancing back down he saw that the Director's aunt had come out of the kitchen and was busying herself at the reception desk. Catching his eye she waved good night.

'Watch it, Pamplemousse,' he thought. 'Watch it.'

The bed in his room had been made up for the night. The sheets and counterpane turned back. A softer pillow replaced the round, hard sausage that had been there when he first arrived. It had been fluffed up to make it more comfortable and inviting.

He put the *tisane* down on the floor beside the only armchair and crossed to the French windows. The doors were ajar behind drawn curtains, but the shutters were closed, making the room feel airless despite the cooling down after the heat of the day. He decided to open them for a while, at least until it was time to put Pommes Frites to bed.

Outside all was quiet; the shops and houses mostly shuttered like his own room. In the time it had taken to reach the upper floor via the kitchen dusk had fallen. Apart from the lights of the hotel, the only illumination came from the Sanisette below.

He glanced down at it and as he did so he gave a start. Something very odd appeared to be happening to the roof. At first he thought it was a cat and then he decided it was the wrong shape; it was much too tall and slender, more like a rolled umbrella. It looked like—it couldn't possibly be, of course, but it looked as if a long loaf of bread was sticking out.

Even as he watched, it rose higher in the air and began waving to and fro like a short-sighted elephant reaching up with its trunk for some out of reach delicacy.

Turning back into the room he made a dive for his working case. A moment later he was back on the balcony again, focusing his binoculars in the direction of the toilet. Issued by *Le Guide* to its staff so that they could furnish reports on the scenery while on their travels, they were normally set at infinity, but at last the object he'd been searching for swam into view.

He'd been right; it *was* a loaf of bread. To be precise, a *baguette*. A *baguette* which, at the very moment of coming into sharp focus, disappeared from view again into the depths of the Sanisette. For a moment or two he held the glasses in position, wondering if the wine at dinner had been more potent than he'd bargained for, or whether he was experiencing the first symptoms of a response to his gastronomic experiments, a blurring of his senses, but he knew what he'd seen.

Pommes Frites eyed his master sleepily as he leaped over the lion's head and dashed past him for the second time in as many minutes. Normally he would have been only too pleased to join in the fun; it would have been an automatic reaction. Give him someone or *something* going at speed and he was after it like a shot—the faster it went the more he liked it. But like his master, Pommes Frites was beginning to feel the after-effects of the meal. He decided that for the time being at least he would remain on the alert, ready to follow on behind at a moment's notice if required, but until that moment he would attend to his own needs. He had other, more pressing matters on his mind.

Outside in the square Monsieur Pample-mousse gazed in growing frustration at an illuminated orange sign on the side of the toilet. It bore the word OCCUPE

He banged on the stainless steel door with his fist. *'Ouvrez la porte!'*

The silence was unbroken and absolute. He tried again. At least whoever was in there couldn't get away. Somewhere behind him he heard a shutter being opened and a light came on from an upper window.

Reaching into his trouser pocket he found a one franc coin and tried inserting it in the slot, but the machine refused it immediately.

He studied the instructions on the side. A time limit of fifteen minutes was imposed. After that the door opened automatically. Given the fact that the present occupant must have been inside for at least five minutes, possibly more, he shouldn't have long to wait.

For a moment he was tempted to call up for Pommes Frites, then he decided against it. He'd made enough noise already. He didn't want to waken the whole village.

Almost immediately he received proof that he'd made the right decision. There was a click and a soft whirring noise as the half-round door began to slide open.

To his surprise a figure dressed from head to foot in black appeared in the opening.

'*Pardon*, Madame.' Automatically, as he stood back a little to give her room, he went to raise his hat before realising he wasn't wearing one. Bent double, a shopping basket clasped behind her back, she sidled past without answering.

He hesitated, wondering whether or not to challenge her, but with what and on what grounds? Perhaps the toilet was in great demand that night?

Determined to get to the bottom of the matter he decided to try his luck with the franc again. Once more it was refused. This time doubtless because the machine was going through its cleansing cycle. Thank goodness he hadn't been taken short. He bent down to re-read the instructions and as he did so there was a sudden flurry of movement from behind. Before he had time to react something heavy struck him a vicious blow on the back of the head. Over and above the jarring sensation in his brain, he was aware of the sound of running feet, and then, as he clawed at the empty air in a vain effort to stop himself from toppling forward, everything went black.

——4——

Pommes Frites at Large

THE REST OF that night passed in a series of fits and starts, a montage of events and impressions which came and went, merging with each other like the opening of an old newsreel. He vaguely remembered coming round and finding himself lying on the cobblestones outside the toilet. They had felt surprisingly damp until he realised it was his own blood. Somehow or other he'd managed to stagger back to the hotel where he must have passed out again, for the next thing he could recall was finding himself sitting up in bed with a jacket round his shoulders.

He remembered being irritated by all the questions everyone kept throwing at him; looking in vain for Pommes Frites, then for his binoculars. He'd been very worried

about his binoculars. They were Leitz Tri-
novids belonging to *Le Guide*. Madame
Grante in Accounts would not be pleased if
he reported them missing. He'd had trouble
enough when he'd lost the cap on the 50mm
lens of his camera. With the kind of wild
logic given only to those who have to deal
with other people's expenses, she had de-
manded double payment. One for the cap
he'd lost, a second for its replacement. In
the end he'd bought a new one himself to
avoid any further argument.

After that he must have dropped off to
sleep; a drugged, dream-filled sleep from
which he struggled awake every now and
then to the sound of dogs howling. Once or
twice he thought he recognised Pommes
Frites' bark amongst them, but each time
he fell back into instant dreams; dreams
which were mostly to do with being chased
by people armed with huge loaves of bread,
bread which always turned out to be made
of stone like ancient clubs.

When he finally woke the sun was high
in the sky. He lay where he was for a while,
allowing his mind to grapple as best it could
with the facts at its disposal; the strange
surroundings, the events of the night before
and the reason for his being there; then he

looked at his watch. It was nearly eleven thirty. He'd slept for well over twelve hours. Such a thing hadn't happened in years.

The shutters over the balcony doors must have been left open from the previous night, for the sunlight illuminated the room with a translucent glow through the thin curtains.

Climbing out of bed he crossed the room and pulled them apart. The sudden shock of the sun straight in his eyes caused him to wince. In the square below a woman with a shopping basket who was about to enter the *boucherie* nudged her companion and pointed up at him. The other woman put a hand to her mouth and said something, then they both laughed.

Turning back into the room he looked at his reflection in a tall mirror next to a chest of drawers and realised for the first time that he was completely naked. His head was bandaged and he needed a shave.

On his way to the bathroom he saw with relief that his binoculars were lying on top of the leather case. His clothes were neatly folded over the chair, his jacket carefully draped over a hanger suspended from the wardrobe door handle, otherwise everything was as he'd left it when he came up from dinner the night before.

Ten minutes later he was lying in the bath, the water almost up to his chin. He wished he'd thought to bring some bath salts with him. The room was devoid of any of the free gifts one had almost come to expect; a sachet of *bain moussant* would have gone down well at that moment. Apart from anything else the surface of the bath had a rough feel to it, the result of years of scouring with coarse powders. He wondered idly if it was the very same bath the Director had suffered in as a child. It was hard to picture a tiny Director covered in cigarette ash.

The thought together with the chilly water made him get out sooner than he might have done, and fifteen minutes later, shaved and freshly groomed, he made his way downstairs, but not before making the surprising discovery that the rest of his clothes—the ones that had received the soaking in the *bidet*, had been pressed and put away in the wardrobe. The shirt was carefully arranged with a piece of pink tissue paper between the folds. The trousers were hanging from a rail.

When he reached the hall he found the

Director's aunt talking to an elderly man carrying a black bag. Even without a stethoscope round his neck he looked every inch the country doctor.

They both seemed surprised to see him.

'Shouldn't you still be in bed?' Madame Louise reached for a chair.

Monsieur Pamplemousse held up his hand in polite refusal. 'I am perfectly all right, thank you.'

'Nevertheless . . .' The doctor motioned him to sit. 'It is as well to be on the safe side. Last night you were anything but all right.' Taking an instrument from his case he lifted Monsieur Pamplemousse's eyelids, first the left and then the right, peering at them closely with the aid of a spotlight. 'You have no difficulty in focusing? No loss of vision?'

Monsieur Pamplemousse went to shake his head and then thought better of it. Doctors were like dentists, they asked you questions under circumstances when it was difficult to reply.

'No vomiting?'

'Not that I am aware of.'

'Good. There are no signs of concussion. They would have appeared by now.' The doctor stood back. 'You've had a lucky escape.'

'What happened?' Madame Louise looked at him anxiously. 'We had a shock when you came back after your walk. Were you attacked?'

'Poof!' Monsieur Pamplemousse brushed the question to one side, trying to make light of it. 'It was nothing. A slight accident. I went to use the Sanisette and I must have tripped and fallen awkwardly.' For the time being he had no wish to discuss the matter with anyone until he'd marshalled his thoughts, least of all with the doctor or Madame Louise.

'I feel it is all my fault.' The Director's aunt sounded weary, as if the whole thing was yet another nail in her coffin. 'I should have warned you about the toilet on your floor. The door is always jamming shut. I keep telling Armand to fix it. There is another on the floor above. As for that monstrosity outside in the square, it has been a source of trouble ever since it was erected. No good will come of it.'

'You had breadcrumbs in your wound!' said the doctor accusingly. He made it sound like a major crime; an act of self-degradation. 'If it was some kind of attack then the police must be informed.'

Monsieur Pamplemousse decided it was time to change the subject. 'I have very little memory of what happened. All I recall is waking up in bed, but how I got there is another matter.'

'You have this lady to thank,' broke in the doctor.

'And Justine. I couldn't have managed you by myself. Getting you up the stairs was hard enough, but then lifting you on to the bed and undressing you.' Madame Louise blushed. 'We couldn't find your pyjamas.'

'They were under my pillow,' said Monsieur Pamplemousse. Somehow the thought of being undressed by Madame Terminé aroused mixed feelings. He was glad he hadn't known about it at the time.

'Oh! But . . .' She looked as if she was about to say something and then changed her mind. 'You must be hungry. You haven't had any breakfast. Let me cook you something. An omelette perhaps?' She turned to the doctor. 'An omelette *fines herbes* wouldn't hurt would it, Docteur Cornot?'

The doctor closed his bag. 'On the contrary.'

Monsieur Pamplemousse's heart sank. He didn't want to hurt Madame Louise's feelings, particularly after all she had done for him, but he had a clear mental picture of what any omelette cooked by her would be like. To begin with the eggs would be over-beaten so that they would start off too liquid, then it would be over-cooked; hard in the centre and not *baveuse*. The herbs would have been added to the mixture beforehand, not whilst it was cooking, so that little bits would have stuck to the pan and much of the flavour lost.

A thought struck him. 'Do you have any large potatoes?'

'Yes, but . . .'

'Put two in the oven to bake. There is a recipe I know. *Oeufs à la Toupinel.*' His mouth began to water. It was a long time since he'd eaten it. It was not something one normally encountered in restaurants.

'In the meantime I must go and look for Pommes Frites. While I am gone you could perhaps prepare me a sauce Mornay if that isn't too much trouble. I forgot to inflate Pommes Frites' kennel last night. If he's been out all night without shelter he will not be pleased.'

The doctor held out his hand as he made to leave. 'On the contrary, Monsieur, if your dog is a large bloodhound, and I assume that is the one since he is a stranger to the village, then the last time I saw him he was looking very pleased with himself indeed. Somewhat worn out, but undoubtedly pleased.'

'Pleased?' Monsieur Pamplemousse repeated the word nervously. 'Why? What has happened?'

Madame Louise caught the doctor's eye. 'I'm afraid Pommes Frites is in disgrace. We have had to put him in the stables out of harm's way awaiting the arrival of the *vétérinaire.*'

'The *vétérinaire?*' Monsieur Pamplemousse felt his heart miss a beat. 'Where is he? I must go to him at once.'

Doctor Cornot picked up his bag. 'There is nothing wrong with him. At least nothing that a good night's sleep won't cure. Although that is not to say it will stay that way. There are those in the village who would wish to see him *coupé.*'

'*Coupé? Pommes Frites coupé?*' Monsieur

Pamplemousse's voice was a mixture of surprise and indignation.

'Last night while you were asleep he went on the rampage. Hardly a *chienne* escaped his attentions. I hesitate to bandy numbers about, but it must reach double figures at the final count. I am not saying that in the final analysis all were unwilling, but as far as I can make out they were hardly given the choice.'

'*Merde*!' Monsieur Pamplemousse's thoughts raced ahead as the doctor's voice droned on. Clearly Pommes Frites had had an attack of the Bernards. A bad one by the sound of it. But why? To the best of his knowledge they had eaten precisely the same thing. Perhaps it was a question of quantity? On reflection, out of purely selfish motives he had been more than generous with the *tourte au lapin*. But that would have been more likely to bring on an attack of indigestion rather than the other. Perhaps it was a matter of certain ingredients affecting only certain metabolisms. What was sauce for the goose was an aphrodisiac to the gander. He resolved to have a quiet word with the *vétérinaire* to see if he could recall any similar happenings in the past. In view of the amount of custom Pommes Frites must have generated for him he could hardly refuse to give an opinion.

'I will go and put the potatoes in the oven.' Madame Louise turned to leave.

'Thank you. And please . . .' He suddenly felt embarrassed at criticising everything she did, but there were certain things that needed to be said. 'Would it be possible to have some *proper* bread with it?'

There was a moment's hesitation. 'I will send out for some.'

'Don't worry. I will go.' He sensed a sudden constraint and realised that for some reason he was treading on dangerous ground. In any case it gave him an excuse to visit the *boulangerie*. One way and another it was getting high on his agenda.

As he said goodbye to the doctor and stepped outside the hotel a woman with a red setter on a lead waved at him from the other side of the square. Monsieur Pamplemousse quickened his pace. The dog appeared unwilling to go anywhere near the hotel and the woman had to drag it along the pavement, so that he reached the *boulangerie* before her. For a moment or two he thought she was going to follow him inside.

'*Une ficelle, s'il vous plaît.*' A *baguette* would really be too painful a reminder.

While the girl was reaching up for his bread he cast an eye over the window display, hovering between a *tarte aux pommes* and a *tarte aux fraises.* Through the glass he could see a small crowd beginning to collect outside. Word must have travelled fast. He ordered two *tartes aux pommes.*

'Is Monsieur in?'

'*Non, Monsieur.*' The girl wrapped the *tartes* quickly but expertly into a pyramid shaped parcel, as if they were a Christmas present. 'He has finished his second baking. Besides, today is Wednesday.'

It was said without offence but the inference that he should have known these things was unmistakable.

Thanking her, Monsieur Pamplemousse paid for his purchases, collected the change, then took a deep breath as he turned towards the door and braced himself for the onslaught to come.

'*Assassin!*'

'*J'accuse!*'

'Poofs' and cries and counter-cries greeted his exit from the shop.

'*Treize! Treize chiennes* in one night.' A man with a golden labrador pushed his way to the front. 'It is *répugnant*. He is a menace to society. He should be *coupé*.'

'And his owner with him!' shrieked a woman who looked as if she couldn't wait to carry out her threat personally.

Monsieur Pamplemousse drew back and held up his hand. 'I protest!' he exclaimed. 'What right have you to say such things? It could well be a case of mistaken identity. How dare you make accusations based on *évidence circonstancielle*.' Privately the thought crossed his mind that thirteen was an unlucky number. Perhaps Pommes Frites had run out of targets.

'*Évidence circonstancielle! Évidence circonstancielle!*' The man looked for a moment as if he was about to have a fit.

'In the dark,' said Monsieur Pamplemousse mildly, 'one dog is very like another.'

'In the dark, Monsieur, *oui!*' The man reached into an inside pocket and withdrew a photograph which he held up and waved triumphantly for all to see. 'But by flashlight, *non!* There is nothing *circonstancielle* about that one's *membre*. *Substantiel* would be the word, and for the use to which he is putting it!'

A murmur of approval went round the group.

'May I see that?' Monsieur Pample-mousse reached out and took the picture from the man. As he looked at it his heart sank. The clarity of the polaroid image was such that it would have brought tears of joy to the eyes of its inventor, Doctor Land. On the reverse side of the coin it would have caused even the most skilled of defence lawyers to furrow his brow in dismay had he been unfortunate enough to undertake the case of Pommes Frites versus The Rest.

The legs which supported him to such good purpose in the picture would not have kept him upright for more than a second in a court of law. Even a plea of diminished responsibility would have been thrown out on an instant. It was very clear that Pommes Frites knew exactly where he stood with his responsibilities and what he was doing with them. Had he been one for singing, he would undoubtedly have been giving voice to the words of the Hallelujah Chorus.

Monsieur Pamplemousse was suddenly and irresistibly reminded of a remark he'd once heard attributed to that famous English man of the theatre, Noel Coward. It had been made when he'd encountered a similar situation while taking a small godson out for a walk in the country.

'The one below has lost his sight,' he'd explained, in one of his flashes of instant wit. 'And the one on top is pushing him all the way to a home for the blind.'

'It is no laughing matter, Monsieur.' The man snatched his photograph back.

'On the contrary,' said Monsieur Pamplemousse firmly. 'In my opinion most things are a laughing matter when looked at in a certain light. The gift of laughter is what raises man above the beasts in the fields. When did you last see a cow laugh? Or a sheep?

'As for Pommes Frites,' he assumed his most conciliatory manner, 'you are absolutely right. He must not be allowed to go unpunished. Were he able to write I would insist on letters of apology all round. To seek pleasure in life is one thing. To obtain it at the expense of others and without their permission is totally inexcusable.'

Taking advantage of the sudden change of atmosphere brought about by his audience having the rug withdrawn from under their very feet, Monsieur Pamplemousse set about beating a hasty retreat before they had time to reply.

'Do not be too hard on him, Monsieur,' a voice called after him as he pushed his way through the crowd.

When he reached the stable at the back of the hotel car park he found Pommes Frites fast asleep in some straw. He might not have received the gift of laughter, but if the seraphic smile on his face was anything to go by it would have been an unnecessary embellishment.

He toyed with the idea of raising his voice in rebuke for the benefit of the others, then thought better of it. That would have been an unnecessary gilding of the lily. He had no wish to tread on Pommes Frites' dreams. Clearly they were giving him much pleasure.

Closing the stable door carefully so as not to disturb him, he made his way towards the back entrance of the hotel. On his way past a second stable he heard a rasping sound and glancing inside saw someone bent over a bench filing the end of a piece of copper piping clamped in a vice. It was the same person he'd seen dodging out of the way when he'd first arrived. Perhaps he had come to do the plumbing in his room. Just outside the back door to the hotel an old woman sat on a stool, a bucket by her side, head bent, hard at work peeling some vegetables. Like the plumber she offered no response to his greeting. For a moment the thought crossed his mind that perhaps she was the one who had come out of the toilet the night before. He dismissed the idea as quickly as it came. She was much too frail. Whoever had attacked him wielded a fairly hefty punch. What used to be known in the force as a bunch of *cinqs*.

Upstairs in his room again he put the binoculars back in the velvet-lined compartment of the case and then locked it. Although there was nothing in there to connect him with *Le Guide*, there was no point in taking chances. He hesitated for a moment or two over his notebook and then slipped it into the secret compartment of the trousers hanging in the wardrobe before making his way back downstairs.

Entering the kitchen he nearly bumped into Madame Terminé who was bustling in the opposite direction carrying a pile of dirty laundry. He held the door open for her. Did his eyes deceive him or was she regarding him in a new light? There was a kind of intimacy in her glance which he hadn't noticed the night before. Already, although he had only been at the hotel for one night he

106

could sense a change; a feeling of tendrils reaching out and taking root. In normal circumstances it would have been a clear signal to move on. Familiarity was not encouraged by *Le Guide.* Familiarity could cloud the judgment.

The Director's aunt was busy by the stove. She, too, looked up and seemed to greet him as an old friend rather than as a client. She was wearing a freshly starched white apron and her hair was noticeably tidier than he remembered it earlier that morning. He judged she was perhaps ten years younger than himself. Perhaps in her mid forties. At times she looked much older.

'Are you sure these potatoes are what you want? It doesn't seem a very good way to start the day—especially after what happened.'

'On the contrary.' Monsieur Pamplemousse looked round the kitchen as he spoke, taking it all in; the *batterie de cuisine* above the long cupboard between the stove and the window—a row of burnished copper pans hanging up, and close to them an array of knives of all shapes and sizes. Beyond that again a selection of *marmites* and casseroles, some old and richly worked, others new and hardly used. Fish kettles and enamelled iron *terrines* completed the picture. Whatever else she lacked, Tante Louise certainly wasn't short of equipment. He suddenly realised he was starting to think of her as 'Tante' rather than plain 'Madame.'

He glanced down at the stove. It looked clean and serviceable if a trifle large for the amount of work it was called on to do. High above it some early eighteenth-century potholders hung from a large beam. They, too, looked clean and dust-free without the greasy surface one might have expected.

'On the contrary,' he repeated. 'The potato is much maligned. Can you think of another vegetable with so many virtues? The potato goes well with everything. It is never assertive. Full of goodness, but never boring. It can be boiled and baked and sliced and fried. Above all, although it is with us the whole year round you never get tired of it.

'Besides, what I am about to prepare is not just a potato. It is a dish fit for a king. I shall need some butter and cream, nutmeg, ham—preferably lean, and it will need to be finely minced. Breadcrumbs and Parmesan cheese. Then I shall need some eggs for poaching.'

While he was talking he reached up and took a *couteau d'office* from the rack on the wall, feeling its blade as he did so. It was a Sabatier, five inches of high quality carbon steel, but it was blunt, sadly and undeniably blunt. Not only that but it was badly stained. Cutting into the potato would transmit an unwholesome taste.

'Do you have any lemon?'

While he was cleaning the blade he felt Tante Louise watching him. 'You seem very at home in a kitchen. You must do a lot of cooking.'

He sought for a suitable answer. It was true to say he felt at home in the kitchen. His time with *Le Guide* had not been wasted. He'd lost count of the number of hours spent watching others at work; marvelling at the expert way they dealt with even the most mundane of tasks. In the right hands even the chopping of a carrot became a work of art. But as for cooking itself; Doucette usually frowned on his excursions into a kitchen which was common property most of the time but became *hers* whenever he used it. Like the Director's aunt, ownership changed according to circumstances. Accusations of using up every pot and pan within sight were rife and not without reason. In the kitchen he became the *gros bonnet;* the big hat, the boss of all he surveyed.

He gave a non-committal shrug, wondering how best to broach the subject of sharpening the knife without causing offence. But in the event he needn't have worried. Tante Louise was only too willing to acknowledge her inadequacies.

Reading his thoughts as he looked around she opened a drawer and handed him a steel. 'Why is it sharpening knives is always considered man's work. I have Madame Camille's son, but he is more of a problem than a help. I wouldn't trust him with them.'

Monsieur Pamplemousse supposed she must be talking of the man he'd seen earlier. Come to think of it, there was a family likeness. 'Have you never thought of getting married?'

For some reason the Director's aunt coloured up. She crossed to the oven and opened the door. 'The potatoes are ready.'

'In that case,' Monsieur Pamplemousse took the hint, 'perhaps you would be kind enough to prepare two poached eggs.'

Removing the potatoes from their rack, he grasped the newly sharpened knife and cut a hole in the top of each. Scooping out two-thirds of the inside of each potato with a spoon, he began mashing it in a bowl along with the butter and cream, adding salt to taste and then a pinch of nutmeg.

Replacing the mixture in the potatoes, he left a cavity in the top of each into which he poured a teaspoonful of the Mornay sauce and another of the freshly minced ham.

'Eggs, please. Now some more of the Mornay.

'Breadcrumbs . . . grated Parmesan . . .' He felt like a surgeon carrying out a delicate operation. 'Can you put the rest of the butter in a saucepan to melt?'

Adding a few drops of the melted butter he placed the potatoes carefully on to a heat-proof dish and put them back into the oven to brown.

'Ça va.' He wiped his hands on a cloth, realising he should have worn an apron. It was just like home. At home he always forgot an apron until it was too late. He looked at her shyly. 'Since I seem to have made free with your kitchen, perhaps you would like to join me? We could share a bottle of Vouvray. It will go well. Unless . . .' he decided to leave the ball in her court. 'Unless you are too busy?'

'There is no one else for lunch. That would be very kind. I will ask Justine to fetch the wine.'

While she was gone he quickly opened the oven door again, breathing a sigh of relief at what he saw. Despite his air of confidence it was many years since he'd last cooked *œufs à la Toupinel*. The result was eminently satisfactory, exactly as he remembered it; golden brown and sizzling in its juices. He hoped it would live up to its looks. In the end it was always the simplest dishes that were the best. He'd once conducted a survey among the great chefs, the ones who'd been awarded three Stock Pots, to see what they ate when everyone else had gone home, and they all said the same.

He loaded up a tray and carried it proudly into the dining-room, almost regretting for a moment that it was empty. It deserved an audience. Even Madame Terminé would have been better than nothing; or Pommes Frites. He wondered what Elsie would have thought of his efforts. Somehow he felt they would have met with approval. Pommes Frites would certainly have got up to have a closer look. For a moment he toyed with the idea of fetching him in, but decided against it. If there was any left over he would take it out for him afterwards. Apart from anything else he wasn't sure if Pommes Frites would totally approve of his little *tête-à-tête;* jealousy might creep in, although given the events of the previous night he could hardly kick up too much fuss. All the same, it was better to be safe than sorry.

A table had been laid for two just inside the door, as far away from the window as possible. The bread, freshly sliced, was in a basket in the middle alongside an empty flower vase. No doubt the Director's aunt didn't want the whole world to know she was lunching with one of the guests; with the *only* guest in the hotel.

Tante Louise made a grimace at the other tables as she entered carrying a wine bucket with an already opened bottle clinking against the ice inside. 'It will be different later in the week—I hope. Friday is the day of the annual *Foire à la Ferraille et aux Jambons* and the village will be *en fête*. There will be a parade and lunch outside in the garden so that everyone can watch. I hope you will still be here.'

The Iron and Ham Fair apart, Monsieur Pamplemousse felt sure he would still be there. The way things were going the Fair would have come and gone long before he'd even begun sorting things out.

He broke off a piece of bread and popped it into his mouth while he was serving. It had the characteristic, slightly sour taste of a genuine *pain au levain*. The inside was airy and cream coloured, slightly chewy. The village baker must be one of a sadly dying breed who cared enough for his art to use a chunk of dough from the previous day's baking as a starter, rather than do it the easy way with yeast. He probably used stoneground flour as well. No wonder the shop was often crowded.

The Vouvray was a contrast in taste; fruity and yet bone dry, with an underlying firmness which came from the Chinon grapes. Overall there was an acidity suggesting a year which lacked sun. It should have been drunk and not kept. Compared with the wine he'd been served the night before it was disappointing. A glance at the label confirmed his suspicions.

'I know what you are thinking. I'm afraid I know nothing of wine.' Tante Louise took the glass he had just poured. 'I have to rely on the judgment of others. I inherited the cellar from my father, and he inherited it from his father before him, but I'm afraid neither of them passed on their taste buds when they died. They both spent most of their time abroad and when they came home they always made up for lost time, squandering what was left of the family fortune —if it ever existed. Grandma swore it did, but no one ever found it.'

The words were said without any trace of bitterness, but Monsieur Pamplemousse pricked up his ears, adding a visit to the cellars to his growing list of things to do at the earliest opportunity. It sounded intriguing.

Photographs of an imposing, moustachioed figure—presumably the grandfather—adorne the walls wherever you looked. He seemed to be forever posing against a tropical backcloth with a glass in one hand and an outsize rifle in the other, his right foot placed firmly on whatever animal had been unfortunate enough to cross his path. Size had clearly been no passport to mercy; large and small, all were doomed to an untimely death. No wonder the local taxidermist had flourished. He wondered how they'd all been transported home. Come to that, how he'd managed to travel with such an enormous cellar. Had the Chablis been served at jungle temperature? And had the champagne exploded after all the shaking about? Or had there been hordes of native bearers weighed down by some gigantic ice box?

He suddenly realised Tante Louise was talking.

'I hope you don't mind my asking?'

'Of course not.' He wondered what he'd let himself in for. 'I shall be only too happy.'

'It seems a strange thing to ask of a guest and you must say if it interferes with your writing, but perhaps it may give you some ideas.'

Monsieur Pamplemousse gave a start. He'd forgotten about his 'writing'.

'Once this week is over things will settle down again.'

'Yes. Er, what would you like me to do?' He put on his thoughtful look, the one he assumed when he was weighing pros and cons.

'Just to be there and offer advice really. I wouldn't expect you to do any manual work, but the more time goes by the more I realise there are so many things I don't know about. I want so much to succeed. The Hôtel du Paradis has been in the family for generations. To lose it now would be like breaking faith with all those who have gone before. Mama, Papa, Grandmère . . . that's her picture on the wall.'

Monsieur Pamplemousse followed the direction of her gaze and dwelt on a gilt-framed picture hanging on the wall beside the bar. He'd noticed it without paying a great deal of attention over dinner the night before. He saw what Tante Louise meant. Grandmère did not look the sort of person one would wish to break faith with; not if one believed in an afterlife and possible recriminations. Even in repose there was a firm line to the jaw and an upward tilt to the head which denoted strength of purpose. With Grandpa away on safari for months on end she'd probably had plenty of time to develop it.

'Sometimes everything seems to be going well and then, for no reason at all, it comes to nothing. We have been in guides and out of them again. I do not understand the reason. I have a niece who is married to someone very important in Paris—an old family friend in fact. I have written to him several times, but he is always too busy. He sends messages to say he is in conference.' Monsieur Pamplemousse knew the feeling.

'Once, a little while ago, there were some men from Paris. They arrived one night in a large, black American car and made offers. When I refused they threatened.'

'What sort of offers?'

Madame Louise blushed. 'Offers I would not wish to repeat.'

'And then?'

'I put something in their soup. They never came back.'

Monsieur Pamplemousse wiped his plate carefully with some bread and then speared the last remaining crust of the potato with his fork. It was the best part, crisp and earthy to the taste, wearing its goodness on its sleeve. Despite her slightly helpless manner, Tante Louise had obviously inherited some of her Grandmère's toughness. She would be a force to be reckoned with. Yet again, he was reminded of the Director's words.

'If those men come again,' he said, 'tell them Pamplemousse sends his regards.'

Before there was time to reply he rose to his feet, removed the serviette from his collar and dabbed at his lips. 'Now I must leave you. I have to go into Tours. Thank you for the meal. Although I say it myself, a King could not have eaten better.'

'And I feel like a Queen. It was delicious.'

He paused at the door, a twinkle in his eye. 'If I am to be your consort, may I offer some advice?

'For a *village fleuri*—a *village* moreover which is about to be *en fête*, your rooms are singularly lacking in colour. Flowers are like women; they are not born to blush unseen.'

Conscious that his step was a little lighter than usual, Monsieur Pamplemousse made his way towards the front door, then changed his mind and headed towards the back entrance. He may have emerged the victor in his encounter with the local inhabitants earlier that morning, but there was no sense in tempting fate.

The old woman he'd seen in the yard outside was no longer there. She must have finished her chores. The paving had been washed down, the table scrubbed. Two bowls and a bucket were placed neatly on a shelf, ready for the next day.

After the shade of the dining-room the sunshine was dazzling. He glanced in at the first stable. The door was still open but the old woman's son was no longer there. As he neared the second stable his pace quickened. Pommes Frites would be awake by

119

now, wagging his tail with pleasure at seeing him. He wished now he'd managed to save some of the lunch for him. The previous night's activities would have whetted his appetite. If his total score bore any relation to it he must be starving. It would be no use pretending he hadn't had any lunch. Pommes Frites' sense of smell was too good for that. In any case he knew from past experience it would be impossible to look him straight in the eye without registering guilt.

Taking a deep breath, Monsieur Pamplemousse paused in the doorway so that he could take full advantage of standing with his back to the light, preparing himself for the onslaught of the fifty or so kilograms of welcome he expected to receive.

But if to expect nothing is to be blessed, then conversely Monsieur Pamplemousse's chances of entering the Pearly Gates at that moment would have received a severe jolt; the whistle that had formed on his lips died away as, like Tweedledum and Tweedledee before him, answer came there none. The normally ubiquitous Pommes Frites was conspicuous by his absence.

Idiotically, he almost found himself looking for some kind of note. Reaching down he felt a compressed patch in the middle of the pile of straw. It was cold to the touch. Tucked away inside it lay a half-eaten bone.

Whatever had caused Pommes Frites' absence must have happened some while ago and been of an unexpected nature. It took a lot to part Pommes Frites from a bone once he'd got his teeth into it. To abandon one altogether pointed to something very pressing indeed.

Perhaps he'd had another of his uncontrollable urges. Worse still, perhaps he was stuck with them. Like some kind of migraine they would keep coming back without warning. His heart sank at the thought. Doucette would not take kindly to the idea, nor would the eighteenth arrondissement.

Feeling deflated and suddenly very much alone, Monsieur Pamplemousse glanced towards the entrance to the car park, noted with relief that the street outside was deserted, and then made his way slowly towards his car. It was time he set out for Tours. No doubt all would be revealed in due course. It usually was with Pommes Frites, and it was no good being impatient.

Pressing the starter he put the 2CV into gear, let in the clutch and began moving off. Almost immediately he became aware

121

that something was amiss. There was a lack of response and the steering felt sluggish. It took a matter of seconds to absorb the facts, marshal them into some kind of logical order and reach a solution. He drew up by the side of the road.

Climbing out again he did a circuit of the car, gazing at the wheels with a mixture of mounting anger and frustration. *'Sapristi!'* Intended to run with a pressure of 1.4 kilograms per square centimetre at the front and 1.8 at the rear, all four Michelin X tyres were as flat as the proverbial *crêpe*.

He looked around for help, but St. Georges-sur-Lie was closed for lunch. The *boulangerie* on the other side of the road was shut, its blinds drawn to keep out the sun. The van which was normally parked at the side was nowhere to be seen.

Faced with such a situation, lesser men might well have resorted to violence of one form or another, kicking the wheels, attacking the bonnet with their bare fists, or even bursting into uncontrollable tears.

Monsieur Pamplemousse did none of these things. Calmly and methodically he removed the keys from the dashboard, selected the second one on the ring, and after unlocking the boot, withdrew a large metal cylinder, little realising as he did so that he was setting in train a series of events which later that same week would save him from a particularly shocking and unpleasant demise.

------5------

Swings and Roundabouts

FIFTEEN MINUTES LATER, tyres inflated, hands and nails freshly scrubbed following a visit to his room, camera equipment on the back scat in case he came across a particularly rewarding view—one that would merit a *jacinthe* or a pair of binoculars in *Le Guide*—Monsieur Pamplemousse set off in the direction of Tours, joining the N152 near Langeais so as to hug the north bank of the Loire. Chameleon-like, its luminous colours reflected the mood of its surroundings and the sky above as it sparkled its way towards Saumur. Watched over by sand martins diving to catch the occasional fly as it wound its way lazily in and out of the dozens of golden sandbanks exposed by the low water, it was still a river to respect. It might have seen grander days but it was a river of sudden whirlpools and currents. You took it for granted at your peril. The occasional tree root sticking up out of the water acted as a reminder that in winter, when heavy rain fell over the Massif Central, it could become a raging torrent in a matter of hours, with anything up to six thousand cubic metres of water heading westwards towards Brittany and the Atlantic Ocean every second of the day.

As he slotted himself into the stream of traffic heading east Monsieur Pamplemousse reflected, not for the first time, on the wisdom of a belt and braces approach to life he'd acquired through his years in the Paris police.

Tubeless tyres were undoubtedly a great invention—until they went down, when blowing them up with a foot pump was an impossibility. All the same, the carrying of a cylinder of compressed air was a needless extravagance in many people's eyes. Madame Grante's, for example. How often in the course of a lifetime did one have need of it? Nevertheless, without it he would still be sitting outside the Hôtel du Paradis waiting for a garage mechanic to turn up.

For the time being at least he preferred to gloss over the fact that the prime reason for carrying a cylinder was so that he could blow up Pommes Frites' inflatable kennel when he went to bed at night. Doing it by mouth was hard on the lungs; worse than blowing up a packet of balloons at Christmas. Pommes Frites' kennel was a large one—king size. He wouldn't be best pleased if he knew his cylinder was empty.

It seemed strange driving along by himself. It was the kind of outing Pommes Frites would have enjoyed, and Monsieur Pamplemousse found himself keeping a weather eye open for likely spots where they might have stopped while he took photographs and Pommes Frites had a run. On the other hand Pommes Frites would probably have ignored the danger signs and gone in for a swim. That would not have been a good idea. Some of the invitingly white sandbanks—the *sables mouvants*—could be death traps.

One thing was certain. If Pommes Frites had gone in for a dip the heat inside the car would have dried him off in no time at all. Monsieur Pamplemousse felt tempted to roll back the roof and then thought better of it. In his present condition the hot sun on his head would not be a good idea.

One way and another there was a lot to

think about. Paris suddenly seemed an age away. It was hard to believe that it was only three days since he'd sat listening to the Director pouring out his tale of woe, and watched Elsie pour out the Armagnac. He wondered if she was still surviving or whether she had moved on. Elsie would probably survive wherever she went. She was one of nature's survivors. He could have done with her help at the hotel, for already a plan was beginning to form in the back of his mind. It was a plan which he knew would tax his culinary powers to their limit, for he was only too well aware that his job for *Le Guide* was merely that of a critic. More often than not it was a case of the legless trying to teach an athlete how to run. No one ever erected a statue to a critic, still less a food inspector.

Buildings came into view, followed by a road junction. Turning right at the Place Choiseul he joined the line of north—south traffic crossing the river by way of the Pont Wilson and entered the rue Nationale. Another day, another time, he might have turned left and booked a table at Barrier just up the hill; the coolness of the courtyard with its fountains would have been a welcome relief.

Spring and late autumn were the best times to visit Tours. Now the atmosphere was humid; a combination of the freak weather and a lack of air brought about by its existence in an alluvial hollow. To the left lay the old city, ahead and to the right the vast area rebuilt after the war. It was hard to believe, sitting in a near-stationary traffic jam on a hot, cloudless day, that nine thousand inhabitants had died during the first bombardment and later during the liberation. Twelve hectares of the city razed to the ground. Hard to believe too that Balzac had once praised the street where he was born as being 'so wide no one ever cried "make way"'.

The thing about aphrodisiacs, one of the points he remembered trying to bring out in his article, was that in many cases success or failure lay in the minds of those who used them, just as some people set out to get drunk and achieved their objective rather quicker than those who were determined to stay sober. To some extent it was psychosomatic—an association of ideas, moonlight helped, moonlight, roses and the right words.

Joining the queue to turn right into the Boulevard Heurteloup, he found a parking space opposite the P.T.T. and climbed out. As he went to cross the road a small blue van suddenly appeared as if from nowhere, missing him by a hair's breadth. The driver seemed to be looking for a parking space too, and it was with an uncharitable feeling of pleasure at having commandeered the last one that he eventually reached the other side and made his way into the building.

A large and satisfactorily fat official-looking beige envelope awaited him. On the back was the familiar logo of *Le Guide;* two *escargots rampant.* He was glad he'd taken the precaution of having it sent *poste restante.* The Director's aunt would have put two and two together and made five in no time at all.

It wasn't until he was on the outskirts of Tours again, heading westwards along the D7 on the south side of the Cher, that he remembered the cylinder of compressed air. He'd meant to replace it while he was there. He glanced in his mirror to see if there was any possibility of doing an about turn and decided against it. There was a long string of traffic nose to tail, a large Peugeot—all jutting-out mirrors and periscopes, towing an outsize caravan, a lorry laden with sand, two more cars, and . . . he snatched another quick look and was just in time to see a small blue van nudge its way out on to the crown of the road in an attempt to see if the way ahead was clear for overtaking. It disappeared again. The driver had evidently decided it wasn't.

Monsieur Pamplemousse looked around. To the left lay the first of the great mushroom caves of the region, carved out of the soft Tufa rock; to the right, beyond a line of poplars, the Cher. The nearest bridge would be at Langeais, soon after it joined the Loire. He decided to play it by ear, seizing the first opportunity that presented itself.

It came sooner than he expected. At Villandry, a car in front slowed momentarily to avoid a pedestrian crossing the road outside the great Chateau which dominated the area. Anticipating a gap in the traffic coming the other way, he took his left foot away from the brake pedal and pulled hard on the handbrake, turning the steering-wheel at the same time. The car spun round! It was a trick he'd learnt while on attachment to the Mobile Squad. It looked more spectacular than it actually was. He'd tried it out once before in the Ardèche. Pommes Frites, who'd been asleep in the passenger seat at the time, hadn't spoken to him for days afterwards. The 2CV rocked as he brought it to a halt in a space between two trees, then it sank back on to its suspension with an almost audible sigh of relief. Horns blared and a succession of irate drivers made gestures at him through their open windows; he could almost hear the 'poofs' which went with the shaking of arched wrists and the thumping of foreheads. Children's faces pressed against rear windows stared back at him as they disappeared from view. The lorry driver, a Gauloise clamped tightly between his lips, tapped his forehead and gave him a pitying look as he drove past. He probably thought the bandage was the result of a previous attempt to do an about turn. Behind them all came the van. It must have been one of millions and yet there was something disquietingly familiar about it. The driver was looking away from him. He relaxed as it went on its way. It was probably nothing, a coincidence . . . and yet . . .

The gravelled area outside the Chateau was crowded with sightseers. The café on the far side looked as if it was about to burst at the seams. Between each gap in the trees on his side of the road there were parked cars as far as the eye could see. Once again he'd been extraordinarily lucky in finding a space.

Grabbing his camera case and the envelope, Monsieur Pamplemousse locked the car and waited for a gap in the traffic, hoping to reach the entrance before a coachload of American tourists.

If Pommes Frites had been with him he probably wouldn't have bothered. More than likely *chiens* would be *interdits*. As he remembered them, the gardens were a dog's paradise; a wondrous sixteenth-century maze of three hundred year old lime trees and boxwood hedges intermingled with flowers and vegetables and crisscrossing paths forming a mathematically precise and harmonious whole which was quite unique. Above it all stood an ornamental lake feeding innumerable fountains and streams which in turn led to a moat surrounding the Chateau itself. The sound of so much water would have played havoc with Pommes Frites' staying powers. The temptation to leave his mark would have been as irresistible as it would have been unpopular.

Once inside, he found an unoccupied arbour near one of the fountains and settled himself down. The contents of the envelope was even better than he'd hoped for. The

Director's secretary had done her stuff. In an accompanying letter she listed the contents.

1. Copy of *L'Escargot*. September issue. (I had to obtain this from Madame Pamplemousse as the file copies were missing and there are no back numbers.)
2. Note from Madame Pamplemousse (attached to magazine).
3. Letter marked '*Privé et personnel*'.
4. *Fotocopie* of entry in Monsieur Duval's diary as requested.
5. Some extra P189's as requested.

He tore open the envelope containing the note from Doucette. It was brief and to the point.

'I hope you want this for the article on page three and *not* the one on page eleven. D.'

It sounded as though the euphoria of their evening out had already worn off. He opened the magazine in order to refresh his memory. The first article, coincidentally was A JOURNEY THROUGH THE LOIRE VALLEY by *L'excursioniste*. That would be Guilot from Dijon. He had a weight problem and was always going on long hiking holidays, coming back worse than when he'd set out. Most of the article was devoted to Savonnieres and its soapwort—still used in preference to modern soaps for cleaning old tapestries. It was followed by a long list of eating places.

The second article was his own. APHRODISIACS: DO THEY WORK OR IS IT ALL IN THE MIND? by A. Pamplemousse! It was longer than he remembered it.

He resolved to send Doucette a postcard. A picture of the Loire Valley. Perhaps he would get one while he was still at Villandry. It would make a change from the usual one of whatever hotel he was staying at and there probably wasn't one of the Hôtel du Paradis anyway.

Putting the magazine aside for future study, he scanned the photostat. It was of a handwritten entry. The background was dark, presumably because the ink had faded and the copy had needed more exposure. The writing was neat and scholarly, as befitted the Founder of *Le Guide;* an ascetic figure whose portrait adorned the wall of the Director's office, viewing all who entered with a stern eye, especially at annual interview time. He looked at the date—August 30th, 1899—a year before the Michelin

133

Guide had been born. History recalled that in those days the Founder did most of his journeyings by boneshaker, an early Michaux. It was incredible to think that he might have travelled all the way from Paris on such a machine. No wonder he had a fanatical glint in his eye. His obsession with *Le Guide* must have been quite frightening, particularly as circulation would have been strictly limited in those days.

He began to read: 'Friday night. Days still hot—but nights getting cooler. Hotel crowded. My room overlooks the square. It is comfortable although the plumbing leaves a lot to be desired.' Some things never changed. 'However, it delivers an adequate supply of scalding hot water of a brownish colour.' Perhaps they did. 'Unfortunately there is a *pissoir* below my window. Neither the sight nor smell can be deemed pleasant.' That, at least, was one thing which had improved. 'Tonight I dined off *huîtres, deux douzaines, truite saumonée berchoux . . .*' He racked his brains. That must have meant it was stuffed with pike forcemeat. The salmon had probably been caught somewhere in the Loire estuary, pink from gorging itself on prawns. *'Lapin aux pruneaux* and *tarte bourdaloue.'* That would have been apricots in millefeuille pastry. 'The *lapin* was over-salt, promoting a strong thirst. Otherwise excellent. A repeat of the previous night. Wine . . .' He went on to list some local names.

Monsieur Pamplemousse closed his eyes for a moment as he tried to picture the scene. They might even have sat at the same table. The Founder would have wanted to be near the window so that he could keep an eye on what was going on outside. He wondered if there had been a Madame Terminé in those days, whisking his plate away before he'd had time to wipe it clean with his bread. More than likely. There had been Madame Terminés all through history.

As for Monsieur Hippolyte Duval himself, he marvelled at his stamina. Two dozen oysters, followed by salmon trout, rabbit, and apricots in pastry—no doubt he'd eaten an equally large lunch that same day, and yet in his portrait he looked the picture of health, as slender as a bean pole. Perhaps it was all the cycling he did. Monsieur Pamplemousse wondered for a moment if he ought to invest in a bicycle and then rejected the idea. Pommes Frites would not take kindly to following on behind.

He glanced down at the sheet of paper

and as he did so his senses quickened. He read the words again.

'I wonder if tonight I shall taste once more the ambrosial delights of the Elysian fields, or was it all a dream?' Something else had been added and then scratched out, making it unreadable.

The following entry, a part of which had been included at the bottom of the page, simply said: 'On to Saumur where I visited the stables of the *École de Cavalerie*. Must return to Paris soon!' There was no mention of what might or might not have happened the two previous nights. No hint of remorse or of hope for the future.

When he'd said 'a repeat of the previous night' did he mean he'd actually eaten exactly the same meal, or was there some hidden meaning? Were the Elysian fields similar to the ones Bernard had discovered, albeit behind the hotel and *sans* the schoolgirls, or was it simply a flight of fancy brought on by a good meal and all the wine. From what little he knew of *Le Guide*'s Founder, he wasn't given to flights of fancy.

The entry put a whole new complexion on things. It could be that the latest happenings were simply a matter of history repeating itself. In which case he must look for a deeper reason. Perhaps there was something in the water? If that was so, why didn't the whole village run amok?

One thing was for sure: the hotel had been vastly more popular in those days with Tante Louise's Grandmère in charge than it was now.

He picked up the envelope marked '*Privé et personnel*'. It was creamy in colour; the handmade paper rough to the touch. Even without opening it he knew whom it was from. The writing was a mixture of styles —on the one hand heavy and sensual, with blotched and corrugated strokes, and yet with very definite repeated loops in the letters 'o' and 'd' indicating deceit. There was no indication as to whether it had been sent to his home address first or had gone straight to the office. Whichever way, if he was the Director he would watch out.

'*Cher ange gardien.*' He wondered how long it had taken her to think that one up. How much time had been spent weighing up the pros and cons of what to call him; rejecting the over-familiarity of Aristide and the formality of Monsieur; trying to find the right phrase. '*Ange gardien*'—he liked it. He wouldn't at all mind being her guardian angel, playing eternal footsies under a table in

137

some heavenly garden. He'd never been called a guardian angel before.

'Please forgive my writing to you but I feel you are the only one to whom I can turn. Please, *please*, can you do something about Elsie? Henri is besotted with her. He has even taken to singing "Rule Britannia" in his bath, and if we have any more of that dreadful pudding I shall scream. Please can you help? It will make me *very* happy. Chantal.'

From a personal point of view it was a thoroughly non-committal note. Although there were a number of lines between which messages might have been read, he searched in vain. There was no hint that she had read his own note. Perhaps that was as well. Perhaps it would never, ever be mentioned. One day it would be found tucked away in a box and people would wonder. At least he hadn't signed it. He consoled himself with the thought that she wouldn't have written at all if she hadn't felt some kind of rapport.

He stood up. Trying to read between lines would get him nowhere. There was work to be done. Time for a quick wander and a few photographs for *Le Guide*'s reference department while he was there.

He looked around for a suitable vantage point and decided to climb some steps leading up to the second level where a herb garden was laid out. Even there his 24mm wide-angle lens failed to take in all he wanted. He backed along a path overlooking the main garden, trying to frame a picture with the pergola on one side and the Chateau on the other. It really needed a helicopter to do it justice. He shifted his position slightly, trying to maintain the verticals and at the same time bring an overhanging branch into shot for foreground interest. As he checked focus on the split image in the centre of the picture his pulse quickened. Towards the middle of the gardens, near where he had been sitting a few minutes before, was a familiar figure.

Slowly and deliberately he lowered the camera and crouched down behind the balustrade. Undoing his bag he took out the narrow angle lens, clipped a tele-extender to it, and changed over from the wide angle. At something like forty metres the nine degree angle of view should give him what he wanted. Switching the exposure to a two hundred and fiftieth of a second to counteract any camera shake, he set the exposure mode to automatic aperture and using the end pillar as a support, stood up, focusing as he went. For a moment he had difficulty in finding what he was looking for then it swam smoothly into view. He realised where he had seen the man before and why he hadn't immediately recognised him. People outside their normal environment and wearing different clothes always took longer to place, even allowing for the beard. Without his white hat he looked just like anyone else. It was the hands that gave it away. The one shielding his eyes from the sun as he scanned the gardens was large and purposeful; a hand made large by the work he did—the constant kneading of dough. It also explained the blue van. It must be the same blue van he'd seen parked near the side entrance to the *boulangerie* the day he'd arrived.

He pressed a button on the base of the camera, allowing the motorwinder to take over while he concentrated on holding the figure in the centre of the frame. Luck was with him. If he'd asked his subject to provide him with a variety of poses he couldn't have been more helpful. Back view, side, fully frontal; the camera clicked inexorably on, recording them all.

The next moment he had gone. Monsieur

Pamplemousse lowered the camera, but the baker was nowhere to be seen. It was probably of no consequence anyway. There was no reason why he shouldn't spend his day off as he chose. On the other hand, the Châteaux of the Loire Valley were for tourists, not for the people who lived in the area and saw them every day of their lives.

He began dismantling his equipment, replacing the standard lens, changing the film. If Pommes Frites had been there he would have sent him off to investigate. Pommes Frites liked nothing better than a good chase. He wondered what he was doing. Even more important, where he was doing it.

As it happened, Pommes Frites was at that moment having similar thoughts, only in reverse. Pommes Frites was wondering what had happened to Monsieur Pamplemousse. He had several important matters he wanted to convey to him. How he was going to communicate them was another matter again, but given the fact that his master was nowhere to be seen the problem didn't really arise.

Having noted the fact that his car wasn't there either, Pommes Frites put two and two together and decided to retire to the stable for the time being where he could finish his bone and bring himself up to date with his thoughts.

There were some, Philistines all, who might have jibbed at the idea of comparing Pommes Frites' brain with a computer, but those who knew him well would have seen the parallels at once.

Admittedly, size for size, there was no comparison. Pommes Frites had rather a large head; a micro-chip would have been but a flea on its surface. Nevertheless, both worked on similar principles, that of reducing everything to a series of questions to which the answer was either 'yes' or 'no'. If the answer to a question was 'yes' it was allowed through. If the answer happened to be in the negative then no amount of knocking, or protestation, or crawling, or appeals to better nature, or name-dropping would allow it through to the next compartment. Pommes Frites had a lot of compartments in his brain and some doors opened more easily to the touch than others, but in the end, as with his man-made counterpart, it was all a matter of correct programming.

That morning, the big programmer in the sky who looked after Pommes Frites' thought processes, had fed him with a great deal of information, all of which had to be absorbed and digested and mulled over before any sort of logical print-out could be obtained, hence the bone.

Given a sudden fall in the electricity supply even the most sophisticated of computers had a habit of printing gobbledygook; lack of bones produced a similar effect in Pommes Frites.

Trails was the subject under analysis. Trails, their origins, destinations and meanings. Pommes Frites had followed quite a few trails that morning. Upstairs and downstairs, in and out of buildings, round and about the village; trails of various kinds, strong ones and faint ones—trails that crisscrossed and merged. There was one trail in particular, reminiscent of a scent he'd picked up outside the Sanisette the night of his master's accident, that was giving him considerable food for thought. There were certain aspects of it which didn't for the moment make sense, and were therefore causing a blockage *en route* as it were, giving rise in turn to a not inconsiderable piling-up of other, lesser pieces of information, each of which had to await its turn in the queue.

Pommes Frites swallowed the remains of

the bone, gave a deep sigh, lowered his problem-filled head carefully between his paws and closed his eyes. In his experience brains, like computers, often worked best when they were left to get on with the job.

Some twenty or so kilometres away, in Saumur, Monsieur Pamplemousse was also having to wait. In his case it was outside a high-speed film processors near the Place de la Bilange. It was a kind of limbo. Unlike Monsieur Duval, *Le Guide*'s Founder, he had no wish to visit the one-time Cavalry School, now the National School of Equitation. If all the posters were anything to go by they were probably getting ready for the annual Equitation Fortnight. Anyway, horses frightened him—he much preferred a wheel at all four corners. For the same reason the Museum of the Horse lacked appeal. The mushroom museum a little way out of town would have been more in his line, but there was hardly time. In the end he decided to go for a wander in the market.

On a sudden impulse he stopped by a *poissonerie* and bought some oysters; four dozen. There was no sense in doing things in a half-hearted way. In Roman times they would have eaten that many with their aperitifs. Casanova was reputed to have eaten fifty or more every evening with his punch. He began to wish he'd ordered more.

Fired with enthusiasm he called in at another shop on his way back to the film processors and bought five kilos of *pruneaux*. If they worked at all it would be enough to inflame a whole regiment.

His enthusiasm for the project in hand lasted as far as the other side of the Loire when he remembered Pommes Frites. Pommes Frites hadn't eaten any oysters. Neither for that matter had Bernard. They wouldn't have been available in August. In Paris, maybe, but highly unlikely in St. Georges, where they would be more conservative about the lack of an 'r' in the month!

Seeing a telephone box, he pulled in at the side of the road. It was time he phoned Bernard.

'What did I eat?' There was a long pause. 'Nothing special. It was a hot day. I was more thirsty than anything. I had a *salade frisée*. That made it worse. The bacon was much too salt. Then I had a grossly overdone *entrecôte*, with some abysmal frites and some more salad, followed by a dreadful *tarte aux pruneaux* . . . hello . . . are you there?'

'I'm sorry. I was thinking.' Monsieur Pamplemousse came back to earth. 'I am working on a theory that it was something you ate. The *pruneaux*, perhaps.'

There was a snort from the other end. 'If you laid prunes all the way from here to St. Georges-sur-Lie and I ate every one of them it would not account for what happened that day.' Bernard sounded aggrieved at being reminded of it all.

'*Courage, mon ami.*'

'That's all very well. *Courage* doesn't pay the bills. My reserves are diminishing rapidly. Already I am having to drink my '75s.'

Monsieur Pamplemousse felt at a loss for words. Bernard was a Bordeaux man, something of a connoisseur. His background was the wine trade and he had connections. If he was drinking his '75s he must be at a low ebb. A thought struck him.

'What did you drink that day?'

'It's funny you should ask. Do you know . . .' Bernard's voice perked up. He'd obviously struck a chord. 'I ordered a half bottle of St. Emilion and when it came— you won't believe this—it turned out to be a Figeac. Beautiful it was too; I remember making notes at the time; soft and velvety and big with it. Much too good for the food

146

and nowhere near the price it should have been. If you ask me they don't know what they're sitting on and most of the people who go there wouldn't know a Mouton-Rothschild from a Roussillon even if the label looked them straight in the eye.'

'Anything else?'

'No. I don't like having too much wine at lunch time. It makes me sleepy. Besides, I didn't get much chance to look at the list. It got whipped away from me by some bat-tle-axe of a female.'

Monsieur Pamplemousse smiled to himself. He wondered what Madame Terminé would think if she heard herself referred to that way.

'I must go now. *Au revoir.*'

'*Au revoir.* And thanks for calling.'

Bernard sounded much more cheerful than when he'd first picked up the phone. Monsieur Pamplemousse wished he could say the same. He felt like a drowning man clutching at straws. Instinct told him that his theory had to be right. Experience told him that finding the answer would mean a lot of hard work. A lot of hard work and a good deal of luck. But luck was something you had to recognise and use when it came your way. Lots of people had their share but failed to capitalise on it.

He put his foot down hard on the accelerator, anxious now to be back. It was almost five o'clock and if he was to put his plan into action in time for the Fair he would need to deliver the shopping with all possible speed. He would also n747ed to be up early the next day. That evening he would have to study his article more fully and refresh his memory. He would need to make out a detailed chart.

Not far from St. Georges-sur-Lie he overtook a long line of caravans and lorries; a travelling circus-cum-fair from Bordeaux. Dark-skinned children watched impassively as he overtook them. The drivers neither helped nor impeded his progress, absolving themselves of all responsibility.

During his absence preparations for the holiday had already got under way in the village. The tricolor hung limply from a pole which had been erected in the centre of the square, bunting joining it to some of the surrounding balconies. Tables and chairs had been set out in the garden of the hotel, ready for the influx of visitors. A white van was parked nearby and a man in blue overalls was attaching some loud-speakers to a branch of the yew tree.

As he turned into the hotel car park he took a quick glance to the right. The blue van was parked in its usual place, although the baker was nowhere to be seen, which perhaps wasn't surprising. He was probably keeping out of the way. He wondered what he would think of the photographs.

To his great relief Pommes Frites was there to greet him, bounding out from the stable, tail wagging, full of the joy of living and of seeing his master again. Quite recovered from his previous night's adventure, he watched the boot being unloaded with interest, then led the way excitedly towards the hotel, dashing here, there and everywhere, investigating and sniffing, looking in the stable adjoining his own and drawing a blank, standing up with his paws on the window sill, peering into the kitchen.

Tante Louise saw him and waved back.

'I have a favour to ask.' Monsieur Pamplemousse handed over his pile of shopping, wondering if in bringing his own food he would cause offence. 'The prunes are to go with the *lapin*. It seemed to me yesterday that if I were to criticise it at all it would be for lack of prunes.'

149

He needn't have worried. The Director's aunt seemed only too pleased. She followed him into the hall and stood at the foot of the stairs as Pommes Frites, nose to the carpet, hurried on ahead.

Monsieur Pamplemousse took his key from her. 'I have been thinking about to-morrow . . .' he said. 'I have some ideas.'

'That's very kind.' For a moment it looked as if she was about to add something, then she changed her mind.

Sensing her embarrassment, Monsieur Pamplemousse came to the rescue. 'I have in mind a *menu gastronomique*,' he said grandly. 'A *menu gastronomique surprise*. If you will allow me the use of your kitchen then together we will prepare a meal fit for the President.'

With a confidence that he was far from feeling, he climbed the stairs and made his way along the landing towards his room. Pommes Frites was waiting for him, scratching the bottom of the door, his excitement unabated. Monsieur Pamplemousse looked at him. There were signs, unmistakable signs.

He reached down. '*Qu'est-ce que c'est?* What are you trying to tell me?'

Pommes Frites lowered himself down

onto his stomach and looked up soulfully. It was the kind of expression which implied that although in many respects the world was a wonderful place, certain aspects of it left a lot to be desired. In short, he had warning messages to convey which meant that all was not well.

Monsieur Pamplemousse slipped the key into the lock, turned it as gently as possible and pushed the door open. The inside of the room was dark, the shutters closed to shield it from the hot sun. Pommes Frites stood up very slowly, remaining still for a fraction of a second while he took stock of the situation, then he relaxed and led the way in.

Following on behind, Monsieur Pamplemousse crossed to the window, unhooked the shutters and threw them open, flooding the room with light. As he did so there was a crackling sound from just below the balcony. It was followed almost immediately by a bellowing amplified voice not far off the threshold of pain, then a raucous burst of music. His heart sank as the noise from the loudspeaker echoed round the square. Sleep would not come easily the following night. No doubt there would be dancing into the early hours.

As he turned back into the room he caught sight of some flowers; a bowl of dahlias standing on a table near the other window. He suddenly felt guilty at having made the suggestion. It couldn't be easy running an hotel almost single-handed, and with the level of custom he'd seen so far money must be tight. Perhaps the problem was self-solving. Perhaps if the Director could hold out long enough his aunt would have to close the hotel anyway.

Aware that Pommes Frites was watching his every movement, he opened the drawers of the dressing table. Nothing appeared to have been disturbed. Pommes Frites didn't even bother to put on his 'you're getting warm' expression; it was all a bit of a letdown. Instead he was wearing his long-suffering, impassive look.

He paused at the spot where he had left his case, the one belonging to *Le Guide*. Pommes Frites began to show more interest. Monsieur Pamplemousse picked it up and examined it more closely. Someone had been at one of the locks. There was a small, barely discernible scratch across the bottom of it. He could have sworn it hadn't been there earlier on when he'd taken the camera out.

Reaching for his keys he opened it and quickly ran through the contents. Leitz Trinovid glasses; the special compartment for the Leica R4 and its associated lenses and filters. Beneath the removable tray was the compartment with all the other equipment; the folding stove and various items of cutlery and cooking equipment for use in an emergency. The report forms were intact inside the lid compartment.

He snapped it shut again. Whoever had tried to open the case had failed. It was a tribute to Monsieur Hippolyte Duval and the high standards he had laid down in the very beginning. If a job was worth doing at all it was worth doing well.

He turned his attention to the wardrobe. As he did so he felt a sudden movement behind him. Turning quickly he was in time to catch Pommes Frites rising to his feet. Tail wagging, a look of approval on his face, he came over to join his master. The signs were clear; he was getting warm at last.

Opening the wardrobe door, he riffled through his pile of shirts and other clothing, then reached out for the single clothes-hanger, feeling as he did so for a tell-tale bulge, knowing at the same time that he would be looking in vain.

His worst fears were realised. The trousers hung limply in his hand, the right side bereft not only of a leg to go inside it, but of any extra weight whatsoever. His notebook, his precious notebook, was no longer there.

Sensing that something was expected of him, Pommes Frites responded. Lifting up his head, he closed his eyes and let out a loud howl. It was a howl which said it all. Monsieur Pamplemousse couldn't have put it better even if he'd tried.

—6——

Alarms and Excursions

GRASPING AN OYSTER shell firmly in his left hand, Monsieur Pamplemousse speared the contents neatly with a fork and twisted it away from its housing, holding it up to the light with the air of a gastronome bent on extracting the last milligram of gustatory pleasure out of the task in hand.

Privately he was wishing he hadn't bought quite so many. He couldn't think what had possessed him. Four dozen! Thirty-seven down and eleven to go. He couldn't remember the last time he'd eaten more than a dozen. Two dozen was the most he'd ever consumed at one time.

Pommes Frites, curled up beneath the table, was being no help whatsoever. He was pointedly ignoring the whole thing, although in fairness even if he had been ready and willing to lend a paw Monsieur Pamplemousse would have thought twice about letting him. For some reason best known to himself, Pommes Frites tended to chew oysters—unlike chunks of meat, biscuits and many other items of food, which often went down so fast they barely touched the side of his throat. In chewing them he usually managed to get the odd valve stuck between his teeth which resulted in a lot of noisy lip-smacking for upwards of several hours afterwards.

He toyed with the idea of slipping some into his napkin while dabbing at his mouth, but decided against it. Madame Terminé was hovering by the bar keeping a purposeful eye on his progress. Nearer still a couple with their heads bent close together were watching his every mouthful with a look of awe. It was too risky.

It was a shame really. There it was, sitting on the end of his fork, a survivor of a family of perhaps one hundred million offspring, the result of a chance encounter by its mother with some floating sperm, left to its own devices at an early age, enjoying its one and only brief period of freedom until the vagaries of the currents off the Brittany coast had caused it to land eventually on one of the white tiles at Locmariaquer where it had spent its childhood until it became old enough and fat enough to be moved elsewhere, to Riec-sur-Belon perhaps, where it had passed the next five years or so, pumping water through itself at an inexorable rate of one litre per hour every hour of its life, surviving attacks on its person by crabs and starfish, and on its already thick and heavy shell by the boring-sponge and the dog-whelk, fighting for the right to its share of food against the rival claims of barnacles, worms and mussels, and for what? To end up unwanted on the end of a fork in St. Georges-sur-Lie! It seemed a gross miscarriage of justice; an unfair return for so much hardship and labour.

He opened his mouth and popped it in, savouring the taste of the sea as it slid down, helped on its way by a cool draught of Muscadet. It was the least he could do in the circumstances.

He wondered for a moment about its sex life. Oysters were reputed to change sex many times; their mating habits were haphazard in the extreme. What, if it ever felt the need, which by all accounts was doubtful, would an oyster use as an aphrodisiac?

The thought produced another. Apart from a feeling of fullness, unwelcome at such an early stage in the meal which, to say the least, was extravagantly conceived, what other effect were the oysters having on him? He gazed across the room at the figure hovering behind the bar. Was it his imagination or was her gaze a soupçon more thoughtful than he remembered it? Did not her eyes appear a little darker, her lips a deeper shade of red? Had not thirty-seven, no, thirty-eight oysters made her breasts appear to rise and fall a little faster as if trying to escape whatever man-made device it was that held them in place? No one could deny that she was well endowed. Nature had not been unkind.

The answer came swiftly. Glancing impatiently at her watch, she was practically on top of him before he had time to gather himself together. Her acceleration from a standing start was impressive.

'Terminé?'

157

'*Non, merci.*' He managed to reach the dish a fraction of a second before her. Picking up a piece of quartered lemon he squeezed it over the remaining oysters before she had time to whisk them away. He must not weaken now.

As if to punish him the salmon trout came on a cold plate, the *lapin aux pruneaux* on an even colder one. It must have been put in the fridge. He found himself reaching automatically for his notebook and then remembered it was no longer there. The thought depressed him.

The arrival of the main course caused a stirring beneath the table cloth, a reminder that Pommes Frites preferred flesh to fish; fish was for cats. As far as Monsieur Pamplemousse was concerned he was more than welcome to his share.

The *tarte* was even worse than he'd feared. To use the word *millefeuille* was a debasement of a language rich in other words which might have been used to describe the pastry. In a pâtisserie contest it would have been a non-starter. *Unefeuille* would have been a better description. *Unefeuille* which had set rock hard and stuck to the plate. Manfully he struggled on.

'Would you like a *tisane?*' With probably

the nearest she'd ever come to registering any kind of emotion other than impatience that evening, Madame Terminé removed the plate and ran a portable cleaner briskly over the cloth. He hoped the crumbs wouldn't jam up the works. There were rather a lot of them. She skirted with practised ease round a lump of cream. 'I could bring it to your room.'

Monsieur Pamplemousse considered both the suggestion and the manner in which it had been made. Was it his imagination working overtime again or was there some deeper meaning in the words. Looked at in a certain light it sounded more like an invitation than a suggestion. *Tisane* and Madame Terminé. The one a sop to the indigestion he felt coming on, the other a definite additive. It could be fatal.

'*Un café, s'il vous plaît.* Here, at the table.'

Unmistakably he had blotted his copy book. Serving coffee at table was not what was uppermost in Madame Terminé's mind at that moment. He glanced round the room. The couple had gone. The only other occupants, a man and a woman in the far corner, were nearing the end of their meal. He'd seen them arrive in a BMW bearing an Orléans registration. He was elderly, florid and overdressed. She was young and plump with a perpetual pout. What his old mother would have classed as 'no better than she should be'. If the amount of champagne they had drunk that night was anything to go by her headache on the way home would be perfectly genuine. Perhaps her escort had heard rumours about the hotel too.

The coffee arrived. It was strong and hot and acrid. He broke a lump of sugar in half and stirred it in, holding the spoon upright for a while to take away the heat. He was anxious for something, anything to take away the taste of the pastry.

It had not been a good meal. Apart from the oysters, which had been as near as possible in their natural state anyway, it had been a thoroughly bad meal. The wine was a different matter. The wine would have been accorded a mention in any guide book. For content, although not for presentation. Presentation was not something the Hôtel du Paradis would ever be noted for. The Bonnes Mares had been delivered and opened without any showing of the label. Madame Terminé had passed the cork briefly past the end of her nose as usual and that was that. Woe betide any man who queried her findings. All the same, had he been there for *Le Guide* he would certainly have made a recommendation for the award of a Tasting Cup, possibly two.

He glanced out into the square. Although he couldn't see it, the moon must be full, for it was almost like daylight. The loudspeaker van had long since disappeared. The Sanisette glowed in a state of readiness. The only other lights came from the *pharmacie* window and what looked like a police car parked outside. Perhaps it was some kind of an emergency. A nudge from below reminded him of his obligations. It was time for a stroll. Undeniably a good idea, but there was a world of difference between thought and execution. He was having difficulty enough rising from the table let alone walking anywhere. Had Madame Terminé's implied offer been genuine and had he taken her up on it the encounter would have been disappointing in the extreme. She would probably have got impatient and cried '*terminé*' before he'd got his trousers even halfway off. As an exercise the meal was a dismal failure. Perhaps Monsieur Duval had gone for a spin in the moonlight afterwards on his bicycle and in so doing had set the various elements in motion so that they merged one with the other to produce a potent and active whole.

As he made his way slowly down the steps of the hotel Monsieur Pamplemousse had to admit to himself that there was very little possibility of that happening in his case. He couldn't remember when he'd last felt so bloated. He now knew what a goose, force-fed to enlarge its liver, must feel like—every day of its life. Slowly he made his way down one side of the square. Pommes Frites would have to make do with one circuit that night, but then one circuit to Pommes Frites was worth more than ten of anyone else's. Nose to the ground he ran hither and thither, pausing every now and then to leave his mark, stopping occasionally to register something more important than the rest. Who knew what plans he was hatching? His nose was working so much overtime it would need more than its weekly dose of vaseline at this rate.

As he drew near the police car a figure detached itself from the shadowy side. *'Bonsoir,* Monsieur Pamplemousse.'

'Bonsoir.' He tried to keep the note of surprise from his voice.

'We heard you were staying in the village.' The remark came matter-of-factly as if it was the most natural thing in the world. Perhaps the information had come from the card he'd filled in when he registered. He didn't think anyone bothered to read them any more, unless there was a very good reason.

He nodded towards the *pharmacie*. 'Trouble?'

The man nodded. 'A break-in. A store-room at the back. It must have happened earlier today but it was only discovered this evening.'

'Did they take much?'

'A few drugs. The usual.' There was a shrug and a brief smile. 'Not a case for the Sûreté.'

'*C'est la vie.*' He returned the shrug. It was the kind of thing that was common enough in Paris, but sad to encounter it in a small village in the Loire. The world was not improving.

'Monsieur has had an accident?'

Monsieur Pamplemousse gave a start, then remembered his bandage. No wonder the young couple in the restaurant had been talking about him.

'It is nothing. It looks much worse than it really is.'

'All the same, Monsieur should be careful.'

Responding automatically to the other's salute, he went on his way, wondering if the remark had been merely a pleasantry or whether it had contained some kind of warning. What with one thing and another St. Georges-sur-Lie was beginning to reveal as many undercurrents and *tourbillons* as the Loire itself.

His feeling of unease lasted all the way back to the hotel. There he paused for a moment at the bottom of the steps, tossing a mental coin, wondering whether or not he would be able to summon up enough breath to inflate Pommes Frites' kennel. He decided against it. In his present condition it would not be a good idea. More than ever he wished he'd remembered to renew the cylinder of compressed air while he was in Tours. His room was hot enough as it was without risking Pommes Frites waking up in the night and climbing onto his bed. Once there he was like a dead weight. On the other hand, another night in the straw might not be a good idea either. Straw harboured insects.

In the end Pommes Frites decided matters for him by bounding on ahead up the steps. It was only too clear where his preferences lay.

As they entered the hotel he heard the sound of an argument coming from the entrance to the dining-room. The man from Orléans was complaining about his meal. From the look on his companion's face he would not be receiving value for money in return for his investment that particular evening. Not even Joan of Arc on her way to the stake could have worn a more heavily martyred expression, nor have had her mind more obviously set on a policy of non-co-operation.

Taking his key from the rack behind the reception desk he caught Tante Louise's eye and gave a sympathetic palm-down shake of his right hand. He would not make a good *patron*. Confronted with such clients he would be hard put to keep his temper, even if their complaints were justified. That would have made him crosser still. There was nothing worse than arguing a case when you knew you were in the wrong.

Opening the door to his room, he reached round the corner and switched on the light. The bed cover had been turned back and his pyjamas laid out with the arms crossed as if in a position of repose.

He glanced into the bathroom. In his absence a large jar of bath crystals had been placed on a small table. He began to feel even more guilty at the way he was taking over things.

He checked the drawers to make sure they were as he'd left them. The single hair he'd left at the side of each was still in place, the tiny mound of talc on top of the wardrobe door hadn't shifted. Nothing had been touched.

Doing his own round of inspection, Pommes Frites looked considerably less confident. His computer was hard at work again, absorbing the evidence afforded by his nose, sifting and sorting it. The more he sniffed the less happy he became. There was a great deal to think about. His pending tray was full to overflowing. He was glad now that he'd insisted on accompanying his master. The adjoining room received his special attention. Several times he went inside and stood with his paws on the edge of the bath peering in like a cat on the edge of a goldfish bowl.

Had Monsieur Pamplemousse been in a more receptive state of mind he would have recognised the signs and perhaps done something about them. As it was, his only ambition was to get undressed and climb into bed. Sleep was the order of the day, or to be pedantic, the night. A drowsiness triggered off by all the wine he had drunk was beginning to take over. Aided and abetted by far too much food, it was enveloping him like a cloud. Work would have to come later, or to be pedantic again, much earlier. First thing in the morning. There was so much to do, so much to read. There were lists to be prepared. In his mind's cye he'd pictured his room as the nerve centre of the whole operation. The walls covered in charts . . .

In the square outside there was the sound of a car door slamming, then a second door. An engine started up, revved impatiently into life by the driver. There was a squeal of protesting tyres as the clutch was let in much too quickly, then a roar and more screeching as the car disappeared into the night.

It would be an unhappy drive back to Orléans. No stopping *en route* to admire the Loire or any of its many tributaries by moonlight.

Monsieur Pamplemousse lay back and closed his eyes, allowing his mind to drift, wondering what the Director's wife might

be like as a travelling companion, or Elsie
. . . or Madame Terminé. Madame Terminé would have had a job getting into the
2CV. There would be no room for hanky-
panky.

A few moments later the sound of heavy
breathing filled the room. Not to be outdone, Pommes Frites lay down and curled
himself up on the lion-skin rug at the foot
of the bed, resting his chin on his paws in
a way which would enable him to keep a
watchful eye on both his master and the
door. If he was going to do guard duty he
might as well do it in reasonable comfort.

How long he slept was—and Monsieur
Pamplemousse would have been the first to
admit the fact—a matter of academic importance beside the reason for his waking.
Beside the reason for his waking it was of
as little moment as the loss of a grain of sand
might be to the Sahara Desert.

The reason was simple enough; it was a
clear case of cause and effect. The cause: a
chemical reaction brought on by the jux-
taposition of oysters and bread and salmon
trout and sauces and rabbit and prunes and
pastry and wine and apricots and cream and
coffee and other embellishments and con-
diments too numerous to mention. Con-

fined for too long and tiring of each other's company, they were now trying to make good their escape by the quickest route possible. Had he paused to consider the matter, Monsieur Pamplemousse might well have laid the blame fairly and squarely on the subversive activities of the oyster and the prune, but pausing to consider anything other than the rumbling demands of his stomach was not uppermost in his mind at that particular moment. All his senses were concentrated on one objective, and one objective only; the relief of Monsieur Pamplemousse.

Cursing his lack of foresight in not taking a room with a toilet in the first place, fulminating on the idiocy of having a lion's head rug in the middle of the room as he tripped over it and nearly went headlong apologising with a singular lack of conviction to Pommes Frites as he trod on him, he wrenched open the door and made his way along the corridor, balancing as he went the opposing needs of haste and the inadvisability of disturbing still more an already seriously upset status quo.

As he reached the door at the end and tried unsuccessfully to open it, Tante Louise's words in the hall that morning came back to him. It was followed by a feeling of panic. *'Merde!'* He racked his brains in an effort to remember the alternatives he'd been offered the day he arrived. Was the room next to his the one with the hand basin and W.C., or was it *numéro trois?* And if it wasn't either of those then which one could it be? It was a mathematical problem with complications of a complexity he had neither the time nor the inclination to solve.

Seeing a narrow flight of stairs to his right he made a bound for them. Tante Louise had said there was another toilet on the floor above. Logically, the door that faced him as he reached the top of the stairs and turned the corner would be the one he wanted. But logic and plumbing at the Hôtel du Paradis did not go hand in hand.

As the door swung open he clutched at his pyjama trousers, fumbling to do up the cord again as he skidded to a halt. Madame Terminé looked shorter than he remembered her. Perhaps it was the absence of shoes. Her feet and ankles were slim like a young girl's. Her thighs, silhouetted against the light from a small table lamp, were firm and white. Standing with one hand resting on the knob of a brass bedstead, her long hair loose and hanging down her back, her breasts large and firm, the nipples as prominent as if they were fresh from a dip in a mountain stream, she looked for all the world like a Botticelli come to life.

How long they stayed looking at each other he knew not. It seemed like an eternity, but it could only have been for a second or two. Surprise gave way to other emotions. She moved as if about to say something, but before she had time to open her mouth he spared her blushes.

'*Pardon*, Monsieur'. He gave a slight bow. '*Excusez-moi.*'

He was not a moment too soon. Conscious that he'd punctuated his attempt at gallantry in a loud and most ungentlemanly way; at one and the same time a full stop, an exclamation mark, and a long drawn-out series of dots—a signal that it would be unwise to linger, he raced back down the stairs again, hoping she wouldn't take it as a true expression of his feelings.

Pommes Frites gave him a jaundiced look through bloodshot eyes as his master dashed into the room and then disappeared again clutching a franc in his hand. He decided to stay where he was for the time being. Many things were possible, but being in two places at the same time was not one of them.

As decisions went it might not have altered the course of events; events that those who believed in such things would have said were predestined anyway from the moment Monsieur Pamplemousse got into his car in the eighteenth arrondissement and set course for St. Georges-sur-Lie, but it did lose Pommes Frites a ringside seat at their actual fulfilment.

Having lost several seconds fathoming out the security arrangements which protected the occupants of the Hôtel du Paradis from the outside world—no less than three very stiff bolts and a chain, followed by several more seconds grovelling around the cobblestoned square in search of his franc which he'd dropped in his haste, Monsieur Pamplemousse arrived outside the Sanisette.

Thankfully, though not surprisingly, the light was at green, indicating that it was unoccupied and ready for use.

Breathing heavily and with a trembling hand, he inserted his coin in the slot of the electronic cashbox located beside the list of instructions and waited impatiently for the quarter-circle stainless steel suspended door to slide open on its base guide. One of the more infuriating things about living in an increasingly computerised world was that man had to wait for machine, and machines refused to be hurried. It was just the same with the garage beneath his block of flats in Paris. Instead of just driving in you had to break a beam of light and wait while an arm which barred your way was lifted. It usually took up to ten seconds. An eternity if you were late home and in a hurry.

Had there been anyone abroad at that time of night they might well have paused, and having paused wondered what kind of dance Monsieur Pamplemousse was performing. Was it a Gavotte or the Boston Two-Step? Or even the jive? Perhaps a combination of all three, with some jungle rhythms thrown in for good measure as he thumped unavailingly and impotently on a door made silent by a core of fibreglass wool sound-deadening material.

At last there was a whirr of machinery from somewhere inside. Having examined Monsieur Pamplemousse's franc and not found it wanting, the coin analyser sent it on its way and issued instructions to admit him. At the same time two fluorescent tubes mounted above the laminated glass base of the skydome were switched on, along with an air heater in the technical area at the rear, an extractor fan in the roof, and the sound play-back system.

Unmoved by the speed at which Monsieur Pamplemousse entered the public area, the door closed again in its own good time, two air jacks securing it in a locked position. Outside, an orange light came on illuminating the word '*occupé*', whilst in the technical area the heater, having ascertained that the ambient temperature was within the permitted tolerance either side of 19°C as laid down in the handbook, switched itself off.

Having no need for either coat-hook or handbag-hanger, ignoring the hand-basin with its automatic soap and presence-operated warm water dispenser, indifferent to the many and varied items of electronic gadgetry at work on his behalf, Monsieur Pamplemousse sank gratefully into place, offering up as he did so a prayer of thanks.

Given the fact that they were the last coherent words he was to utter for some while to come it was perhaps as well that he addressed them heavenwards. At least it gave him the benefit of having made early contact with the forces of good on high, rather than with their opposite number below, directly connected as the latter were with the Sanisette by means of an enamelled cast-iron drain trap in the base.

Even the least mechanically minded of occupants would have detected a change in the normal pattern of events as a clunking and grinding began somewhere towards the rear.

Monsieur Pamplemousse clutched frantically at the bowl as he felt it begin to tilt, slowly and inexorably turning him head over heels in a backwards direction to the sound of the Grand March from *Aida*. Jamming him doubled-up and powerless to move in the opening behind, it exposed him to the depredations of a high-speed revolving brush, a brush which sought out corners and probed where no man had probed before. The final indignity was provided by a centrifugal pump which completed the cycle by unleashing a spray containing a mixture of water, disinfectants, detergents, germ killers and, for good measure, a bio-degradable anti-fungus agent.

To say that his whole life flashed before him while all this was happening would have been an exaggeration. Forty seconds, however long it may seem at the time, was nothing for one who had led such a long and adventurous life. To say that Monsieur

Pamplemousse spent the time marvelling at the way so much equipment had been packed into such a small space would have been as far from the truth as it would have been to say that he emerged a happier, cleaner man than when he went in. Cleaner, yes. Not since he'd been a babe in arms had he felt quite so cleaned and scrubbed and disinfected. But happier, no.

As he tottered back across the square for the second night running, Monsieur Pamplemousse couldn't remember ever having felt quite so unhappy in his life.

He let himself in to the hotel and crawled up the stairs with but one thing in mind; an overpowering desire to sink as quickly as possible into a very deep bath.

Pommes Frites' look of surprise at his master's appearance changed to one of consternation and alarm when he saw what he had in mind. Jumping to his feet, he began racing round the room like a thing possessed, rolling his eyes as if in the grip of some kind of fever. Then, seeing it was getting him nowhere, he suddenly stopped dead in his tracks and for the second time that day let out a howl, only this time it was a howl of warning rather than sympathy; a cry of anguish not just from the heart but from his very soul. It was the kind of howl that would have caused any members of the Baskerville family, had they been staying at the Hôtel du Paradis, to sit up and take immediate notice before pulling the blankets over their heads in an effort to shut out the noise.

But for the time being at least Monsieur Pamplemousse was too far gone to care. Battered and bruised, smarting all over, still hardly sure whether he was coming or going, standing on his head or his heels, he felt as though he had been passed through a *lavage automatique* backwards. At least in a car wash they posted signs, telling you to retract your aerial and warning of possible damage to badges, wing mirrors and other protruding accessories. Some of his accessories felt as if they had been damaged beyond repair.

Turning off the hot tap he sprinkled the crystals into the bath and then clambered in, sinking slowly back until the water was lapping his chin. Oblivious to all but its soothing effect, luxuriating in its new-found softness, unable to summon the energy to reach up and turn on the heater, he closed his eyes and relaxed.

Pommes Frites eyed his master mournfully for a moment or so, and then he, too, lay back on his rug. He'd done his best. No one could say he hadn't done his best. What happened now was in the lap of the Gods. Far stronger forces than his were needed to cope with a master whose indifference to his fate, whose inability to cope with even the simplest of messages, whose sublime disregard not only for his own safety but for the feelings of others were of such proportions they were almost beyond belief.

—7—

None but the Brave
Deserve the Fair

'I AM SORRY, Monsieur, such a thing is not possible. In any case we cannot accept complaints from the general public. It is necessary to go through the proper channels.'

Monsieur Pamplemousse took a deep breath, counted up to ten, and with commendable restraint, began again.

'Monsieur, I have been through so many channels this morning it makes the Loire look as placid as an *enfants'* paddling pool on a hot day. I have been on to the *Mairie*, and there I have spoken to the *Service de la Santé*, the *Chef de la Salubrité Publique*, the section dealing with the *environnement*, and the man whose job it is to judge the suitability of candidates for the *village fleuri* competitions. All of them have assured me that it is not their responsibility. They none of them wish to know. I have now been in this telephone kiosk for over half an hour getting absolutely nowhere while contributing to its upkeep to the tune of so many francs I have long ago lost count of them, and it is very, very hot. I am speaking to you as a last resort. If I do not get a satisfactory reply I shall catch the next train to Paris where I shall take great pleasure in squeezing one from you, drop by drop. When I have done that I shall make use of my many contacts with the press to make sure that before I call in and see my *Député* while *en route* for my lawyer, the affair which you treat so lightly receives maximum publicity.'

Taking advantage of the momentary silence, Monsieur Pamplemousse poked his head outside the booth and mopped his brow. All around the square stalls and tables were being set up. They had been arriving since dawn, along with battered vans full of junk and delivery vehicles laden with hams

179

and sausages. Smoke rose from a mobile *créperie* and he caught the pungent whiff of cooking oil from a hotdog stand. To say that it was hot inside the telephone booth was the understatement of the year. It felt like an oven, draining reserves of both strength and temper. It was always the same; one contained oneself up to a certain point and then let rip on some poor, unsuspecting individual who happened to be in the wrong place at the wrong time.

'With the greatest respect, Monsieur . . .' the voice was more conciliatory, as he knew it would be. The press had its uses. 'Innumerable precautions have been taken to ensure that such an accident cannot possibly occur. On entering the toilet an infra-red beam detects your presence. Then there is an electronic detector with not one, but two sensitivities. First of all it ascertains if your weight is more than 4 kg, then it checks to make sure that it is more than 25 kg. This happens whether you are standing or sitting. Only when it is happy does the detector allow the door to be closed. On leaving, the door closes and locks automatically, then no less than *three* independent mechanical, electrical and pneumatic systems come into operation to make absolutely certain there is no longer anyone present. Only then, and I repeat, *only* then can the cleaning cycle begin. The floor and the toilet bowl tilt back to be received by the technical area . . .'

Monsieur Pamplemousse fed another five franc coin into the machine. He could see that in no way was it going to be a quick conversation.

'Monsieur,' he began, 'I yield to no one in my admiration for your product. I have acquired an intimate knowledge of its working parts. I know exactly what happens when the cleaning cycle begins. I have, as you put it, "been received" and I bear the scars to prove it. I can see that it is clearly a scientific achievement of the first magnitude. It has raised what is, after all, one of man's most basic and universal and necessary functions to the level of space travel. No doubt the day will come when one of these devices will be sent up on a rocket and landed on the moon for the benefit of any passing astronauts, regardless of race, colour, creed or sex, who happen to be taken short. However in the meantime, last night, here in St. Georges-sur-Lie . . .'

'Pardon, Monsieur, did you say St. Georges-sur-Lie?'

'I did.'

'Aahaaah!' The voice at the other end sounded relieved, as if that one single fact explained everything. 'We have had a certain amount of trouble at St. Georges-sur-Lie.'

'Trouble? What sort of trouble?'

'Sabotage, Monsieur. Sabotage of the very worst kind. Vandalism is one thing. The units are designed to cope with that. They are constructed in architectural grade concrete with a fluted exterior design to prevent unauthorised bill-posting, the internal surfaces are protected by anti-stick paint, the metal parts sand-blasted, metallised and painted. Also, as part of the service, there is a periodical pressurised steam cleaning . . .'

Monsieur Pamplemousse suppressed a sigh and fed in his last five franc coin. Better not to interrupt the flow. It might cause further delays. A girl in a red and gold uniform went past carrying an instrument case. Heads turned, for she was wearing tights and the shortest of skirts, her bottom encapsulated in the briefest of snow-white pants. He wondered idly how old she was. She looked in her early twenties but was probably about fifteen. No doubt she was taking part in the Grand Parade that afternoon. There was a poster on the wall opposite advertising the appearance of a local drum and fife band, led by Miss Sparkling Saumur. He turned his attention back to the phone.

'. . . it was like it right from the beginning. One expects a certain amount of opposition. People are resistant to change. Even in the world of *aménagements sanitaires* there are those who would stand in the way of progress—they prefer the cracked porcelain bowl they know to one made of cast aluminium, enamelled to the highest standards. Others object to paying for something which nature requires them to do at regular intervals whether they like it or not. But this is different. Wires have been cut. Sand has been injected into the mechanism of the door leading to the technical area— we have had to change the lock three times. The sound tape has been tampered with— the music erased and replaced by a voice uttering threats and warnings to anyone using the services. The skydome has been interfered with . . .'

'Who would do such a thing?'

'Poof! That, Monsieur, is anyone's guess. You may well ask. There is no accounting for some people's behaviour. In my profession I could tell you some tales. These units are expensive and they require a minimum number of operational cycles each day to make them viable. This one has been standing idle for over six months.'

'I mean, what sort of qualifications would he need?'

'A knowledge of electricity. The ability to find his way round a circuit diagram. It is not difficult. Common sense—or the lack of it. We will look into the matter immediately, of course . . . although several of our engineers have refused to go there any more.'

Monsieur Pamplemousse saw the remains of his time ticking away on the meter. 'I must go. Thank you for your help.'

'*Enchanté*, Monsieur. Thank you for being so patient and understanding. It cannot have been a pleasant experience. And, Monsieur . . .'

'*Oui?*'

'I trust such a thing will never happen to you again, but should you be so unfortunate, should the impossible occur, you will find there is a telephone installed in the technical area . . .' There was a click and the line went dead. It saved Monsieur Pamplemousse the trouble of explaining that the part of him nearest the technical area had not been the one he normally used for conversing with, although at the time it would have been more than capable of giving vent to his feelings. He replaced the receiver and left the kiosk, momentarily lost in thought as he gazed at the back of the hotel.

Apart from the old woman still eternally peeling vegetables near the back door to the kitchen area, there was no one in sight. He'd been up even earlier than her that morning. It was a good thing he had too, for the car park was now full to capacity and his own car was totally hemmed in. He would never have got to the market.

Pommes Frites was nowhere in sight; he was probably still upstairs, keeping a low profile and catching up on lost sleep. One way and another he must have foregone quite a few hours over the past two nights. Perhaps, dog-like, he was instinctively following the doctor's advice: a darkened room and plenty of water. Monsieur Pamplemousse made a mental note to make sure his bowl got filled up; in the prevailing weather he probably had need of it.

There was a small queue outside the *boulangerie*, but no sign of the owner. He was probably snatching some sleep before his second baking. He'd already been hard at work that morning when Monsieur Pamplemousse went past; smoke rising from the wood-fired oven.

The old woman picked up a bowl and went into the kitchen. Taking advantage of her absence he slipped through the car park, in and out of the cars, and took a quick look inside the stable next to the one Pommes Frites had occupied. It was empty. At the far end, under a window, there was a work bench with a vice, and to one side of it a board with a selection of tools fixed to the wall; a file or two, several screwdrivers of various sizes, some pliers. The bench had been brushed down. A drawer beneath it was fastened by a padlock. It looked very workmanlike, neat and tidy.

Catching sight of something light-coloured on the darkened surface of the floor, he bent down and picked it up. It was a small piece of crust from a loaf. Under the bench was a wire hair grip.

Hearing the sound of voices, he slipped both into his wallet and hurried outside. Pausing for a moment by his car, he pretended to check the wheels before leaving the car park.

Resisting the temptation to buy an old typewriter on the first stall he came to, he hovered over a pair of kitchen scales at the next, wondering if he should get them for Doucette. He had no use whatsoever for the first—it would be sheer self-indulgence; the second would be too late for her birthday, too soon for Christmas, and presents in between were usually regarded with suspicion. He settled instead for a pocket corkscrew. It had the name of a *négociant* from Burgundy engraved on the side and must have been a give-away at some time.

The finding of the crumb had set him thinking. The hair pin too. There was probably a simple explanation for both, and yet . . .

He continued on his circuit, past displays of clothes, past tables clearly belonging to professional antique dealers from neighbouring towns—their owners organised and impassively getting on with their knitting or reading a paper, past other tables littered with open cardboard boxes and trays full of oddments and bric-à-brac; hinges, locks, old keys, cotton-reels—the more useless the item the more hopeful the owner. He stopped by a stall selling old postcards and riffled through them. There might even be one of the hotel. He wondered if Doucette had kept all his cards over the years. If she had there would be enough for her to open a stall of her own by now.

Glancing towards the front of the hotel he saw Tante Louise standing on a pair of steps hitching a row of coloured lights to a branch of the tree. Below her Madame Terminé was bustling to and fro laying the tables for *déjeuner*. He hobbled over towards them, conscious of a certain stiffness setting in.

'May I help?'

Tante Louise looked down. '*Non, merci.* I know where they go. Armand should be doing it. He knows about these things—but he has disappeared.'

Madame Terminé gave a loud sniff as she went past, glancing skywards. He had a feeling that part of her reaction was meant for him; a reproof for what hadn't happened the night before. Hell hath no fury like a woman scorned. He hoped it wouldn't affect her work that day. A lot depended on Madame Terminé's ability to stick to the seating plan he'd drawn up.

'What did she mean by that?'

'Justine? Oh, nothing. It's simply that Armand is a little strange sometimes. It is always worse when the moon is full.' He held the steps while she came down. 'It is very sad. He could have been many things, but no one wants to employ him any more. I only do so because of family ties. He is the son of old Madame Camille who you've seen outside, and if she went I don't know where I'd be. Her mother worked for my grandfather, but as for her husband . . . who knows? There was a lot of family inter-marrying in those days and sometimes it backfired. Armand is harmless enough, but he mixes with strange people.' She picked up the cable. 'I think she is also a little put out over your helping so much in the kitchen.'

Monsieur Pamplemousse looked even more thoughtful as he climbed the stairs to his room. It was like doing a jigsaw. You did the edges first and then started on the middle. Suddenly, from being on the point of writing to the manufacturers complaining that there must be pieces missing, they came to light and a picture began to take shape.

As he'd suspected, Pommes Frites was fast asleep, effectively blocking the doorway to the bathroom. For some reason best known to himself, Pommes Frites had become obsessed with the bathroom. He

189

opened one eye and watched while his master pottered around the bedroom, picking up a piece of paper here, consulting a chart there.

The fact of the matter was, with zero hour approaching Monsieur Pamplemousse was anxious to set the wheels in motion. He looked at his watch for what seemed like the hundredth time that morning. It was barely twelve o'clock. Hard to believe that he'd been up and about and working for close on eight hours. Hard to believe in one sense, easy in another. He suddenly felt inordinately tired as he lay back on the bed and closed his eyes while he took stock of the situation. The idea of serving a *menu surprise gastronomique* had been something of an inspiration; the planning and the execution had taken it out of him. At least it had cured him for the time being of the ambition he'd once had, and still had from time to time, of one day retiring and opening his own small hotel. Like many such ambitions the dream was better than the realisation, but without such dreams what would life be all about? Working for *Le Guide* was probably as good a compromise as any.

All now depended on Madame Terminé

following his instructions to the letter; serving the right dishes to the right tables according to a pre-determined plan so that he could note the effect if any, putting ticks in little boxes. He opened his eyes again and picked up one of the charts. Monsieur le Directeur would have been proud of him. He wondered if anyone since Roman times had organised a menu with so many aphrodisiac variations and possibilities. Bernard would appreciate it. It might even jog his memory. There must be something he'd forgotten.

The apéritif had been his first stroke of genius; the *potage noisette* his second. In one fell swoop he would eliminate many possibilities. He went over the ingredients of both again in his mind, making sure nothing had been forgotten.

The apéritif he'd prepared early that morning, boiling it up first before leaving it in the refrigerator to cool. Red Bourgucil from Touraine, cinnamon—he wondered if perhaps he'd been a little over-generous with the cinnamon, almost two large spoonfuls had gone in—ginger, vanilla, honey, cloves. It should set their red corpuscles going, getting them in the right mood for the *potage:* pounded almonds mixed with the yolks of hard-boiled eggs and chicken stock, then more honey. The cream was a bit of a problem. Strictly speaking he should have mixed it in while he was making it, but according to the researches he'd done while writing his article, the appearance of a bowl of cream on the table was often a great attraction to the female of the species. Ideally, too, he should have added a few pine kernels, perhaps even standing some cones on end; one opposite each place setting. The more phallic symbols there were around the better. Symbols and symbolism ran right through the literature of aphrodisiacs and played almost as large a part as did the ingredients themselves. What was interesting, and what none of his researches had ever told him for sure, was whether, like hypnotism, you could only persuade people to do things they had a deep desire to do anyway, never the other way round.

In the end timing had been one of the chief factors which eliminated many possibilities; timing and availability coupled with intent and the danger involved. The latter had included all the drugs with known side-effects, like mescaline, cannabis, Spanish fly and ginseng, which in any case was too slow-acting to have been the cause of Bernard's problem. For similar reasons he rejected avocado laced with nutmeg—awarded special mention in his article because it was one of the least dangerous. Its preparation required time, implying malice aforethought, and when it acted it was reputed to be a case of lighting the blue touch paper and retiring immediately. Cucumber stuffed with truffles was too exotic.

Whatever it was it had to be as anonymous and taken for granted as the arrival of the *facteur* with the morning mail, as accepted a part of the daily scene in the Founder's time as it was today, innocuous on the surface and yet powerful and long lasting. The length of the fuse was less important than staying power. Bernard must have driven for more than an hour before he finally succumbed; Pommes Frites' staying powers the other night were not open to question.

Uncooked celery stalks—if stories were to be believed—fulfilled most of the requirements. Rich in methaqualone, they were highly prized in some northern countries like Greenland and Norway. Rabbits thrived on them. But it would be unusual to find them eaten raw in large quantities in the English fashion. They would be much more likely to find their way into a salad or be cooked in some way.

It was a problem and no mistake.

Getting up from the bed, he went out onto the balcony. By leaning over the rail he was able to see along to the garden. Already there was a sprinkling of early arrivals. One man was holding his apéritif up to the light, discussing the contents of the glass with his companion. Draining it, he signalled to Madame Terminé for a refill. That was something he hadn't bargained for. He wondered if he'd made enough. More than ever he regretted the loss of his notebook. With its neatly ruled and divided pages it was ideal for keeping records under cover of the tablecloth.

Slightly to his relief, Pommes Frites ignored an invitation to accompany him downstairs. He would have his work cut out keeping track of things as it was without any other distraction. Apart from which, after last night's meal it wouldn't do Pommes Frites any harm to go without for a day.

By the time he arrived in the garden more than half the tables were occupied and Madame Terminé was waving some new arrivals in, uttering cries of *'avancez,'* whipping the serviette off the table and into their laps as they sat down. His own table, arranged towards the back of the garden close to some steps leading down to the cellars, had the double advantage of being in the shade and yet affording a view through a gap in the others so that he would be able to see the parade when it took place.

Putting his Leica and a writing pad on a chair beside him he settled down and looked around. To his right a party of four were already into their soup, rewarding his efforts with a great deal of lip-smacking and comments and wiping of bowls with their bread. He wondered what they would say if they knew why he'd made it. To his right a local was protesting about there being a fixed menu with no choice—demanding that he be told in advance so that he could choose his wine. He received short shrift from Madame Terminé. Madame Terminé was, in fact, in her element. He could see now how how she had acquired her brusque manner; it must have been ingrained in her from the days when the Hôtel du Paradis was always full. With over forty people to serve there was no time for pleasantries; the pace never slackened for a moment. His own apéritif was poured in passing without a drop being spilled nor a hint of anything other than exactly the right measure. Not too little, not too much. His *'merci'* was registered and acknowledged with the barest of nods.

Some more girls went past, walking self-consciously and awkwardly on their high heels, aware that they were being watched by all the people at table and taking comfort in the safety of numbers. They were a motley selection, some barely into their teens, others twice their age. Bottoms of various shapes, sizes and denominations, pert or full, tight or wobbly, turned and faced the hotel as they made their way across the square. Most of them would probably automatically pull their skirts down over their knees if they caught you looking at them in a restaurant or an *autobus,* and yet there they were, as bold as brass, generously displaying thighs and bosoms for all the world to see, their faces lobster red from the combined effects of over-tight uniforms, the hot sun and the comments from the crowd.

'Poor things.' Tante Louise joined him for a moment. 'Fancy having to wear those uniforms in this heat. I must give them something to drink.'

She disappeared into the hotel again and

a few minutes later came out with a jug and a pile of paper cups. He watched as she followed after them like a mother hen.

On the far side of the square he recognised the *gendarme* he'd spoken to the previous evening, on traffic duty now, directing cars away from the area where the band would be performing. People were already starting to form small groups in front of the stalls on either side. Despite the heat, the hotdog stand was doing a roaring trade.

Above the sound of the Fair, which had been building up all the morning—the steady rumble of a roundabout and the cracking of rifle fire—he could hear a staccato roar like the high-pitched buzzing of a swarm of angry bees. It came from a tarmac area just beyond the fairground where later that afternoon there would be miniature car racing. It was the latest craze; radio-controlled toy cars treated with all the solemnity of the real thing. Marshals with their flags. Pit stops. Mechanics in overalls wielding tiny screwdrivers and bottles of benzine, and all the usual hangers-on. From the tree above his head the loudspeaker crackled into life as someone blew into a microphone, then it went quiet again.

Madame Terminé bustled past with the

first of the entrées. He made a quick note on his pad. Table four was getting a selection of open tartlets; eels, *moules, asperges,* accompanied by spinach; table seven was getting frogs' legs, brains, *jambon* with *ananas* and turnip. It was hard to picture turnip being an aphrodisiac. On the other hand Scotsmen ate it with their haggis. They probably had need of it, wearing kilts in all the cold weather they had to endure.

He had never made so much pastry in his life before. One thing was certain; it couldn't be any worse than the stuff they normally served, and it had the merit of making everything easier to organise beforehand.

The Director's aunt came back across the square. Above the other sounds could now be heard the banging of drums and the trilling of fifes. Refreshed, the band was tuning up in readiness for its big moment.

She paused on her way past and put the jug down on his table. 'There's a tiny drop left in case you get thirsty.'

Monsieur Pamplemousse thanked her and picked up his camera, checking as he did so that he'd set it to shutter priority and with a speed fast enough to accommodate the marchers when they appeared. He'd

198

opted for the 45–90 mm Angenieux zoom; a new toy he was trying out on behalf of *Le Guide*. He ran through it. The colour would be slightly warmer than a normal Leitz optic, but at its widest he was able to get a bit of foreground interest with an overhanging branch framing the top of the tree and tables to either side; at its narrowest it was tight enough to be able to get some reasonable groupings on the band when it arrived.

He made another quick note. Table three had just taken delivery of an artichoke tart, kidneys and cream and *foie de veau;* they were looking slightly enviously at the table next to them who were deeply into *escargots, ris de veau* and hare. He decided to keep an eye on them in case they tried to do a swop. That would not be good for his records.

He took a quick glance around. Everything seemed to be normal. It was a scene that was probably being repeated all over France wherever the sun was shining. The tables were full; the conversation animated.

The only abnormal note being struck at that moment, or to be strictly accurate a succession of abnormal notes, came from somewhere beyond the square as the band, having embarked on an arrangement for drums and fifes of 'The Entrance of the Gladiators', set off on its journey.

As the sound drew near, Monsieur Pamplemousse raised his camera, zoomed in and focused on a vertical rod supporting a canvas hood on one of the stalls in line with the centre of the square, then zoomed out again in readiness for the big moment.

He wasn't a second too soon. Intended to be played as a quick-step, the march was being performed in double quick time. Whether the band was trying to keep up with Miss Sparkling Saumur, or whether Miss Saumur was trying to keep one step ahead of the band, was a moot point, but they entered the square at a pace neither the composer, Julius Fusic, nor the organisers of the Fête had ever anticipated. With a rippling motion not unlike that of a giant tidal wave building up and then pausing before making a final plunge at the end of its travels, they came to a shuffling halt facing the Hôtel du Paradis several bars ahead of the final notes.

Monsieur Pamplemousse zoomed in on the leader, trying to hold her image steady in the viewfinder as she bobbed up and down, marking time as if treading the very grapes she had been chosen to represent.

Merde! It still wasn't tight enough for what he wanted. Quickly he changed to a narrow angle lens—the one he'd used at Villandry. Fortunately it still had the two-times multiplier attached. He pulled the jug nearer and rested the camera on top to steady it.

At nine degrees Miss Sparkling Saumur looked rather frightening. Sparkling was not the word he would have used. Miss Fixed-Intensity would have been more apt. Mouth working, hair billowing out behind her, knuckles white through gripping her baton, she seemed to be in the throes of forces beyond her control. Beads of sweat which had collected on her brow formed a tiny rivulet and ran down her cheek. It clung for a moment to her upper lip, then a tongue, long and red and moist, emerged to lick it away, slowly and deliberately performing a full circle as if in anticipation of more to come.

He started the motor drive. With luck it would make a good cover picture for the magazine; a change from the usual landscape or hotel. If only she would stay still for a second. Pressing the rubber cup against his eye he tried hard to hold focus as she filled the frame, first with the whole of her head, then so close he had to sacrifice

201

the top of her forehead in order to avoid cutting off her chin. Her eyes, blue and shining with a kind of intense inner light, seemed to be staring straight into his. He would get Trigaux in the Art Department to process the film for him. It was the kind of thing he revelled in, squeezing the utmost out of a negative. Now he'd lost the chin. Taking his head away from the viewfinder he suddenly realised to his horror that she was heading straight towards him. Not only that but the rest of the band were following hard on her heels, pushing and shoving, their sheets of music falling unheeded to the ground. The drums had taken on a strange rhythmic beat, the few fifes left playing had become shriller, more insistent.

He jumped to his feet and looked around for somewhere to go, but the wall behind him was too high, the tree was without any kind of foothold. On either side his way was barred by the other tables and beyond those to his left he was hemmed in by the crowd in the square. Gazing heavenwards in desperation he had a brief glimpse of Pommes Frites standing on the balcony, looking down in wonder at the sight below, and then they were on him, shrieking, pulling, grasping, clutching, tearing at his clothes like beings possessed of insatiable thirsts and unquenchable desires of a kind no man had hitherto dared name let alone attempt to gratify.

Pommes Frites' eyes grew rounder and rounder as he watched his master disappear down the steps leading to the cellars, lost beneath a heaving mass of arms and brown legs, discarded red and gold uniforms, white knickers, brassiéres, heaving bosoms and tangled hair. It was a scene of such complexity that had Dante been making preliminary notes for his Inferno he would have undoubtedly put them to one side fearing that the critics of the day might have accused him of being over-fanciful.

Pommes Frites turned and hurried back into the room. Pausing briefly at the door, he grasped the handle firmly in his mouth and turned his head. A moment later it swung open. It was a trick he'd learned on his induction course with the Paris police; one which had earned him bonus points at the time, and then later that same year applause from the crowd when he'd demonstrated it at the annual police Open Day.

Over the years he'd had occasion to try it out more than once in the course of duty, but he had a feeling that never before had it been used on a matter of quite such urgency and importance.

8

The Dark and the Light

DOCTOR CORNOT CLICKED open his pen and began to write. 'You are a very fortunate man, Monsieur.'

Monsieur Pamplemousse sat up in bed and glared at him. 'I am *not* fortunate,' he bellowed. 'I am most unfortunate! In the space of three days I have been hit over the head, upended in a Sanisette, and now I have been ravaged by a gang of female musicians. Do you call that fortunate?'

The Doctor tore a piece of paper from his pad. 'I suggest you apply this to the affected parts three times a day. The swelling may persist for a while and there is a certain amount of soreness, which is not surprising in the circumstances. But nothing is irreparably damaged. No bones are broken.'

'*Bones!*' repeated Monsieur Pamplemousse bitterly. 'I should be so lucky!'

'You are not the only one to suffer,' the

doctor continued unsympathetically. 'I have hardly slept since yesterday. Half the members of the drum and fife band are still under heavy sedation. Madame Lorris, their trainer, is in an intensive care unit at Tours and likely to remain there for some while. I fear for her sanity. She had only just recovered from an unhappy experience earlier in the year when she heard voices uttering threats in the Sanisette. Others—the ones who were unlucky enough to be bringing up the rear and so received the full brunt of Pommes Frites' rescue bid—will be unable to sit down for a week. As for Miss Sparkling Saumur, there is talk of her being deposed. I do not care for some of these modern expressions, but to say that she got her *culottes* in a twist would have been all too apt had she still been wearing them . . .'

Monsieur Pamplemousse gave a shudder and held up his hand. 'Stop! I do not wish to be reminded.'

Doctor Cornot picked up his bag and then paused and gazed at him curiously. 'In a sense it is none of my business. My business is to attend to the sick and in that respect one may say that since your arrival in this village business has never been better. I turn a blind eye to many things I see in passing.

If I didn't . . .' he gave a shrug. 'But in this instance I must confess to a certain curiosity. What *did* you give them?'

'*I* gave them nothing,' said Monsieur Pamplemousse firmly.

'Well, someone did. And whatever it was it had exceptional power. Its effects were fairly instant and long lasting. Poor little Hortense is in a dreadful state. She cannot stop moaning and her mother has had to tie her to the bedstead and lock the door. Admittedly she has always been advanced for her age and has been suffering the consequences of late, but . . .'

A thought struck Monsieur Pamplemousse. 'Have there been other "happenings" in the past?'

'Not with Hortense. Her problems are more imaginary than practical. She reads too many magazines and they put ideas into her head. But there have been rumours of "goings-on" from time to time. Not on such a grand scale as yesterday and none that have involved me directly.'

'For example?'

'Stories of people—couples usually—often from outside the area—the locals do not patronise the hotel very much these days, but couples who have come to dine and then, for some reason or other, lost all control of themselves. Sometimes even before they have been able to reach the safety of their cars. There was a case only a few months ago. The police had to be called . . . buckets of water were thrown in Reception. One of the gendarmes got badly bitten when he tried to separate them.'

Monsieur Pamplemousse recalled the couple he'd seen the day of his arrival; two who *had* made the car park. 'Do you have any theories?'

Doctor Cornot gave another shrug. 'Nothing in this world happens without a good reason. From all that I have heard it had nothing to do with alcohol. According to a colleague who attended them they were well below the limit which would have prevented them from driving. They were running a temperature and their pupils were severely dilated, but otherwise there was no trace of their being under the influence of any kind of narcotic. In any case, they were not the type; the girl was a perfectly respectable member of society—a librarian. He was a watch repairer from Chartres. Neither had been involved in anything of the kind before. Ergo, they must have been exposed to something abnormal.'

'Would you be prepared to stand up in court and give evidence?'

'Believing something to be true is one thing. Proving it is quite another matter. To answer your question—no. Anyway, in your case it will not be necessary. After all, you were the one who was attacked.'

'I am really asking on behalf of a friend. A friend who also had a strange experience after dining here. His case comes up soon.'

'In that case, Monsieur, I would look back into history. I would visit the offices of the local newspapers and go through their files for the turn of the century. Consult records. Search for previous happenings. Dig out all the evidence I could find. Then I would advise your friend to get himself a good lawyer.'

'You are saying?'

'I am saying that this hotel has a curious history. My father, whose practice I inherited, used to relate stories of similar occurrences. They had been told to him by his father before him. There was a time when the Hôtel du Paradis enjoyed quite a reputation in these parts. That is how it got its name. Once upon a time it was simply called the Hôtel du Centre. Then, on the death of Madame Louise's grandfather it all stopped;

as suddenly as it had begun. It is only recently—within the past few months—that it has started again.'

Monsieur Pamplemousse lay back and closed his eyes, mentally picturing a photograph on the stairs which showed Tante Louise's grandfather clutching a bottle of claret as he stood with one foot on a rhinoceros carcass. He had a roguish twinkle in his eye and a satisfied air. Come to think of it in most of the pictures there had been one or two native girls hovering in the background. Naked, nubile and with an undeniably contented expression on their faces. It was not beyond the bounds of possibility that on one of his many expeditions to Africa he had stumbled across some secret formula, some witchdoctor's brew, that he'd managed to keep to himself. No wonder he kept making return trips.

'Supposing,' he began, 'supposing there does exist some thing or some combination of things that triggers off this behaviour? A catalyst of great power and intensity. And suppose someone were to discover the secret, what then?'

'I would say that someone would need to tread very carefully,' said the doctor, 'for he would be in possession of knowledge which many men would stop at nothing to own. Such knowledge in the wrong hands could be an easy source of great wealth and power. It is the kind of knowledge men have been seeking all through history. On the surface the begetter of much pleasure, but in practice, as you know only too well, also the cause of much pain, discomfort and misery.

'It did not escape my notice, Monsieur, that just now when you listed your current misfortunes you mentioned that you were hit on the head the night you arrived. It did not surprise me unduly, for the wound was not really consistent with your story of having tripped and fallen over. Nor did you seem over-anxious to report the matter to the police. In passing I asked myself why. Since we live in an area where such attacks are rare, and since robbery was not the motive, the only reason I could think of was that you had accidentally stumbled on something you shouldn't have and that someone was saying very forcibly "Keep off! Do not interfere in matters which are not your concern."'

At that moment the telephone by the side of the bed rang shrilly. Monsieur Pamplemousse lifted the receiver. *'Un moment.'* He held his hand over the mouthpiece. 'Thank you, Docteur. You have given me much food for thought. If I may, I would like to continue this discussion later. It is possible I will have something more tangible to talk about by then.'

Doctor Cornot nodded. 'If that is so, then congratulations. It will be a pleasure. I will come and see you again tomorrow. In the meantime, *au revoir*. Fortunately this time you will *have* to stay in your room otherwise I would add "take care".'

Monsieur Pamplemousse digested the last remark without fully understanding it and then, as the door closed, put the receiver to his ear again. It was Tante Louise.

'There is a long distance call for you. I said you were not to be disturbed but whoever it is insists on speaking to you. I'm afraid it is a bad line. It is hard to understand what he is saying. Would you like me to ask him to call again later?'

'*Non. Merci.*' Monsieur Pamplemousse winced as he reached behind to plump up his pillow and make himself more comfortable. It felt as though every bone and muscle in his body was aching. As soon as he was through with his caller he would ring down and ask someone to take his prescription round to the *pharmacie* for him.

Pommes Frites stirred and looked at him sympathetically over the end of the bed. It was an 'I know exactly how you must be feeling, we're all boys together' look. Had the giving of winks been part of his repertoire of tricks, Pommes Frites would undoubtedly have given his master an extra large one at that moment. Not that Monsieur Pamplemousse was in a particularly receptive mood for such pleasantries. Breathing heavily, he glared at the end of the receiver.

'Who is that?

'*Pardon?*' he repeated. 'I cannot understand a word you are saying.'

Banging the earpiece with his free hand, he tried again. 'Monsieur, I do not know who you are or what you want of me, but I have enough things on my mind at present without having to deal with illiterate idiots. You sound as though you have a handkerchief stuffed down your mouthpiece. If you cannot talk to me properly then . . .'

'Pamplemousse, I *am* talking with a handkerchief down my mouthpiece. I am doing so because I do not wish my voice to be recognised. Now, please let me say what I have to say.'

'*Pardon*, Monsieur le Directeur.' Monsieur Pamplemousse found himself automatically sitting to attention. 'Forgive me, I did not realise . . . you may speak freely. There is no fear of our being overheard.'

'I trust you are right, Pamplemousse. Things are in a sorry state. What was the last thing I said to you?'

Monsieur Pamplemousse racked his brains. He disliked conundrums at the best of times, but clearly the Director expected an answer. '*Au revoir?*' he ventured.

A noise like an explosion came from the other end.

Monsieur Pamplemousse tried again. '*Bonne nuit?*'

'No, Pamplemousse.' The Director appeared to be having trouble in controlling his patience. 'I was referring to the three A's: *Action*, *Accord* and *Anonymat*, but above all, and correct me if I am wrong, Pamplemousse, above all we agreed on *Anonymat*.'

'That is true, Monsieur, but . . .'

'Since you have been at St. Georges-sur-Lie, *Action* appears to be negligible, *Accord* as far as I am concerned is non-existent. As

213

for *Anonymat*—all France knows of your goings-on. It is headline news. Pommes Frites was on breakfast television this morning.'

'Pommes Frites, Monsieur? But that is not possible. He is here with me now. I could reach out of bed and pat him . . .'

'Bed!' thundered the voice at the other end. '*Bed!* Do you realise what time it is?'

Monsieur Pamplemousse groped for his watch. 'But, Monsieur, I still do not understand . . .'

'Have you looked outside your hotel recently, Pamplemousse? Your *balcon* is being watched by millions. Ever since Pommes Frites was seen peering through a gap in them, the colour of your curtains has been discussed and analysed and photographed. I'm told they have achieved the highest ratings since the World Cup. No doubt by courtesy of satellite, Pommes Frites and your curtains were also seen by millions in San Francisco and Peking as well. Do you call that *Anonymat?*'

'*Excusez-moi*, Monsieur. *Un moment.*' Letting go of the receiver and regardless of his condition, Monsieur Pamplemousse jumped out of bed and rushed to the window, pulling the curtains to one side as he went. Almost as quickly he dropped them again. Clutching the window frame for support, he took a moment to regain his composure before trying again, this time through a much smaller gap.

But if he'd been hoping that like a mirage the view would have disappeared he was doomed to disappointment. Overnight a great change had come over the square. Gone were all the stalls and vans which had arrived for the fête. Their place had been taken by other vehicles, making it appear, if anything, even more crowded. In front of his room, pointing straight towards him from the top of some scaffolding, was a television camera. Even as he watched a red light came on and the operator pressed his face to the viewfinder as he took a firm grip of the panning handle. On the ground below another man wearing headphones was supervising while a man disgorged a small mountain of other equipment; two more cameras, tripods and lights. Cables snaked their way across the cobblestones towards a mobile control room. Men in jeans and checked shirts and girls with clip-boards added to the bustle. A mobile canteen had replaced the hot-dog stand. On the roof of the Sanisette, surrounded by empty beer cans, a man crouched holding a Nikon camera with an ultra-long-focus lens. By his side stood a battery of other lenses.

In the centre of the square, watched by a small knot of interested spectators, he recognised Miss Sparkling Saumur being interviewed in front of a second television camera. In direct contrast to her uniform for the parade, she was soberly dressed in a long black skirt, a white blouse done up to her neck and low-heeled shoes. Taking a handkerchief from her bag, she dabbed at her eyes as she turned to point with her other hand in the direction of the cellar steps. The floor manager stopped her for a moment, gave her a comforting pat, and then asked her to do it again using her other hand. Something to do with the light no doubt. A make-up girl stepped forward and dabbed at her forehead. The producer was obviously squeezing the most out of the situation.

Very slowly Monsieur Pamplemousse made his way back to his bed, climbed in and picked up the receiver again. He had to admit that *anonymat* was not the word he would have used to describe the scene outside.

'I'm glad you agree with me for once,

Pamplemousse. At least we have achieved some *accord*. I tell you, the press this morning does not make pleasant reading. It is like Bernard all over again only this time it is even worse. Do you know how many?'

'I was not in a position to make an accurate count, Monsieur.'

'Over forty.' The Director sounded gloomy. 'The youngest was six years old, the oldest was seventy-three. All victims of your uncontrollable lust.'

'With respect, Monsieur. It was not they who were the victims, it was I.'

'That is not what the journals are saying, nor the television.'

'I have the scars to prove it, Monsieur. I can get a certificate from the doctor.'

'I do not wish to hear about them, Pamplemousse. And who is Madame Toulemonde?'

Monsieur Pamplemousse racked his brains. The Director was in one of his darting moods.

'She is selling her story to *Ici Paris*. They are advertising it already under their "coming attractions". Soon the presses will be turning.' There was a rustle of paper. 'Blonde, thirty-nine year old Madame Justine Toulemonde. "How I Fought Like a

Tigress to Retain My Honour.' She says she was attacked by you in her room two nights ago. You were like a man possessed. It was only her training with the Resistance Movement that saved her.'

'A complete and utter fabrication, Monsieur. If I was possessed of anything it was an urgent desire to visit the toilet. I had a bad attack of the *douleurs*. If she was attacked in her room she must have kept her eyes closed for it was not I.'

'She says you have a mole on your left knee. Do you have a mole on your left knee, Pamplemousse? I can easily check with your P.27.'

'*Oui*, Monsieur, but I can explain. She must have seen it the first night I was here, when she was undressing me. I had been hit on the head by a *baguette* . . .'

Monsieur Pamplemousse held the receiver away from his head as a spluttering sound came from the earpiece. Pommes Frites watched sympathetically as his master gazed towards the ceiling waiting for the noise to subside.

'That, Pamplemousse, is the most unlikely story I have ever heard. I knew there would be a woman at the bottom of it. I said to Chantal only last night, mark my words, always with Pamplemousse there is a woman at the bottom of things. *Cherchez la femme.*'

'What did your wife say, Monsieur?' asked Monsieur Pamplemousse uneasily.

'Never trust a man with loose shoes.' The Director sounded puzzled. 'I can't think what she meant.'

'There is no reading the female mind, Monsieur. Women are beautiful creatures. They have qualities which in many ways make them superior to men, but I sometimes feel that when the good Lord created them he must have reached a point when he sat back, wondering if he had not been a little over-generous with his gifts, that perhaps enough was enough. It was at that point he must have decided to take away their sense of logic in order to help balance the scales. It makes them say strange things at times.

'As for Madame Toulemonde, if she is as inaccurate with her forthcoming revelations as she is with her present pronouncements, then we have nothing to fear. She is neither a natural blonde—that I can state categorically—nor will she ever see thirty-nine again—a fact which does not require the use of an electronic calculator to verify.

If she received her training in the Resistance Movement then even at *forty*-nine she would have needed to attend unarmed combat lessons in her pram.'

Taking advantage of the momentary silence at the other end, Monsieur Pamplemousse pressed home his advantage. 'How are things *chez vous*, Monsieur?' he ventured. 'How is the young English *mademoiselle*? What was her name? Elsie?'

From the even longer silence that followed he knew he had scored a direct hit. A direct hit and a diversionary move at one and the same time.

'*Chez nous*, things are not good, Pamplemousse. *Chez nous*, I would say things have never been worse. There have been ultimatums. Zero hour is approaching fast. What with that and Bernard, now this, I am beginning to wonder where it will all end.'

'I am glad you rang, Monsieur,' said Monsieur Pamplemousse with a confidence he was far from feeling. 'Despite all you may have read and heard, I have not been idle. Progress is being made. I do not wish to go into details at present, but I hope soon to be in a position to render a full report.'

'I hope so, Aristide. I hope so.' The Director's voice sounded full of gloom. 'If they are not then we will need to add a further "A" to our list. "A" for *Adieu*. In the meantime I will give you another.'

'Monsieur?'

'*Allure. À toute allure.* There is no time to be lost.'

Monsieur Pamplemousse replaced the receiver on its cradle and lay back for a moment. Talking to the Director had left him feeling quite exhausted. It often did. It was like playing squash with at least six opponents. Balls came at you from all directions. One moment reaching a high, then next moment down in the depths.

He climbed out of bed again and crossed to the window. As he made a tiny gap in the curtains and peered through he saw the red light come on over the lens of the camera opposite his window. Someone in the control room must be glued to the monitors. The technicians were probably on permanent standby, waiting to record any and every movement.

Making his way to the door, he opened it and tip-toed across the landing. He could hear voices below and as he peered over the bannisters he caught a glimpse of two men sitting on the bottom stair. One of them had a camera slung round his neck.

Back in his room he slipped the bolt and then slumped into the armchair. It was all very well for the Director to say make all possible speed, but how? He couldn't have been more heavily guarded if he'd been incarcerated in a top security prison. No doubt the back stairs were being watched as well. It was like being in a state of siege. For a moment he toyed with the idea of adopting some kind of disguise. The chances were they didn't know what he looked like—apart from a general description, and from past experience he knew how widely they could vary. Clearly they didn't have his name. The Director would have made a point of it if they did. Tante Louise must have hidden the register. He was tempted to telephone down and ask her to come up. She might have some ideas. Then he abandoned the thought. She was probably being watched as closely as he was, her every conversation listened to. Gun mikes would be trained on his window.

He wished he could reach outside and close the shutters. The heat was really getting intolerable. Although there was a stillness in the air, his pyjamas felt wringing wet; his bed looked uninvitingly dishevelled.

Stretched out on the rug, Pommes Frites resembled a late-night reveller who'd abandoned all hope of getting home and decided to doss down on his astrakhan coat instead. He envied him his ability to shut out the world, letting its problems take care of themselves. The biggest crisis in his dreams was probably a drama called 'The Great Bone Robbery'.

Glancing round the room, he saw that someone had rescued his camera and bag of equipment. From where he was sitting it looked remarkably undamaged; a tribute to Leica. Perhaps when it was all over he would write to them. If Hasselblad could make capital out of their cameras being sent to the moon . . . His note pad was missing, but he'd hardly managed to write anything on it anyway.

He closed his eyes. There was no chance whatsoever of getting any sleep. He had far too much on his mind. But the rest would do him good. What was needed was some kind of diversion. A distraction of major importance. One which lasted long enough to take everyone's mind off the job in hand so that he could make good his escape. One which . . .

It was dark when Monsieur Pamplemousse came to again. Forcing himself awake he climbed unsteadily to his feet, nearly tripped over the recumbent form of Pommes Frites, and made his way to the bedside table. Strange, but it was still only six o'clock by his watch. He crossed to the window and slowly parted the curtains. The sun was hidden behind a layer of haze. In the sky above there were banks of cumulus cloud. No red light came from the camera. Its operator was slumped over a book, his headphones round his neck. The scene in the square was less animated than it had been earlier. Boredom had set it. Now would be the time for action. Later on they would be on the alert again, expecting something to happen. Lights had been rigged up facing the hotel. They were probably ready to be switched on at a moment's notice.

As he turned away from the window Pommes Frites rose slowly to his feet. It was a ritual awakening, performed in a time-honoured manner. First there was the stretching of the back legs, the lifting of the rump in the air, then came the stretching of the forelegs, outwards as far as they

224

would go, usually followed by a rippling motion which started at the rear and made its way slowly but inexorably towards the front as muscles were brought back to life. Last of all came the pushing forward and slight raising of the head, coupled with the closing of the eyes; prelude to a yawning return to normality.

On this particular occasion Pommes Frites' head made momentary contact with its opposite number attached to the rug below, giving an effect in the darkened room not unlike a mirror image in a pool, and as it did so Monsieur Pamplemousse suddenly had one of his blinding flashes of inspiration.

It was a notion which was at once ridiculous and bizarre, eccentric and outlandish, and yet of such simplicity he had the feeling it might just work. It had to work. He would make it work. In all the accounts he had ever read of great escapes through the ages the common factor, the connecting link which ran through them all was the element of surprise. Surprise was the one great weapon the escapee possessed. *Ennui* and the fading light were on his side.

Never one to allow the iron to grow cool once it was in his hand, Monsieur Pamplemousse reached for his suitcase, his issue one from *Le Guide*. Removing the tray which normally carried his camera equipment, then the second which accommodated the emergency cooking apparatus—its contents a miracle of the folding-metal worker's art, he reached into a compartment at the very bottom and withdrew a small leather sachet.

Pommes Frites watched with interest as Monsieur Pamplemousse laid the contents out in a neat row on the floor in front of him; a selection of needles, a hank of thread, a thimble, a tape measure and a pair of folding scissors. Undoubtedly his master was up to something—he recognised the signs, and the enthusiasm, determination and speed with which ideas were being translated into action communicated itself. He wagged his tail. Pommes Frites like a bit of activity every now and then. He'd enjoyed a very good sleep, several very good sleeps in fact, now he was more than ready for action, and although cutting up his bed was not exactly what he would have chosen had he been asked to fill in a questionnaire, he was quite prepared to go along with whatever his master had in mind.

Despite the heat, ever anxious to please,

he didn't raise any objection when Monsieur Pamplemousse wrapped the lion skin round his body, and he happily lay back with his paws in the air while it was sewn into place. Nor did he demur unduly when the head was pulled over his own. Admittedly it made it hard to see where he was going and his growls took on a hollow, roaring sound, but if that was what was wanted, then so be it. Walking wasn't easy; it was more a matter of progressing round the room in a series of leaps and bounds. However, this seemed to please his master out of all proportion to the effort it took. He basked momentarily in the words of praise and the encouraging pats his activities evoked.

'Bonne chance.' With his master's words ringing in his ears he hurried out on to the landing. In the past he had tended to look down on dogs who wore any kind of clothes. There were quite a few of them about in Paris, not so much in the area where he lived, but he came across them occasionally while on excursions further afield. Dogs in coats, sometimes even in plastic boots and hats. He always treated them with the contempt he felt they deserved; not even worthy of a passing sniff. But suddenly, as he made his way down the stairs, he discovered

the change the wearing of any kind of uniform brings about. It was a whole new world. The effect he had on others was electrifying. As he ambled out into the square in a kind of sideways lope people scattered right, left and centre. Women screamed. Men shouted. Somewhere a whistle blew. He broke into a trot, uttering growls of delight. It was all very satisfying. Quite the most enjoyable thing he'd done for a long time.

Upstairs in his room Monsieur Pamplemousse watched Pommes Frites disappear into the gathering gloom with an air of equal satisfaction. He let go of the curtains. Now he must quickly translate deeds into action on his own behalf. It wouldn't be long before the makeshift disguise was penetrated. There wasn't a moment to be lost. Dressing with all possible speed, he grabbed his case and made for the door, pulling himself up just in time as it began to open.

The back view of Tante Louise came into view. She was carrying a tray on which reposed a large jug and a glass.

'I've brought this for you,' she announced. 'It's iced *tisane*. I made far too much yesterday for the girls in the parade and it seems a shame to waste it.'

The Storm Breaks

IN 1856, FOLLOWING a violent storm during the Crimean War which badly damaged the French fleet sheltering in the Black Sea outside Balaclava, Napoleon III charged Monsieur Antoine Lavoisier, a celebrated chemist of the time, to devise a system of weather forecasting which would ensure that such a thing never happened again.

Thus began a series of developments which some hundred and thirty years later led Monsieur Albert Forêt, an amateur weather enthusiast who lived in St. Georges-sur-Lie, to open the door of a slatted white-painted box set exactly two metres above the lawn in his back garden and note that the indicator on a mercury barometer within showed an alarming fall in pressure.

Even as he entered the new reading on a pad, a gust of wind funnelled through the gap between his house and the garage, raising clouds of dust from the driveway on the far side. Simultaneously, a device inside his greenhouse closed the windows automatically.

All of which indicated that an enormous quantity of air was being sucked upwards to a great height, leaving behind a vacuum which, by the laws of nature, had to be filled.

Monsieur Forêt closed the door to his box, made sure the greenhouse was properly fastened, then hurried indoors calling out instructions to his wife to secure all the shutters while he telephoned a friend in the next village who owned a vineyard.

Half a kilometre or so away, Monsieur Pamplemousse took a quick glance out of the Hôtel du Paradis at the now deserted square and then looked up at the sky. The cumulus clouds which had begun to develop earlier had come together, forming one vast towering mass of cumulo-nimbus, the top layer of which had already taken on the ominous shape of an anvil.

'I think we are in for a storm,' he called.

Tante Louise shivered as she led the way down some stairs between the entrance to the dining-room and the kitchen. 'I hope not. I hate thunder. It always makes me feel as if something awful is about to happen.'

'In that case,' said Monsieur Pamplemousse comfortingly, 'the cellar is probably the best place to be.' As he spoke he wondered where Pommes Frites had got to. Perhaps success had gone to his head and even now he was sidling along a bank of the Lie suffering delusions of grandeur, King of the Jungle and all he surveyed. He hoped not. Pommes Frites didn't like thunder either. At home in Paris he usually hid in a cupboard. Hiding in a doorway in St. Georges-sur-Lie would be bad for his image.

As it happened, he needn't have worried, for Pommes Frites wasn't very far away. His mission completed, he was lying just inside the hotel stable with his nose to the ground watching some ants scurrying to and fro, their pace almost twice its normal rate as they sought urgent shelter.

After a lot of thought, he had reached the conclusion that not only was biggest not necessarily always best, but that he'd had quite enough of being dressed up for one day. Just outside the village he'd met a man with a gun. Fortunately shock had affected the other's aim, but it had been a nasty moment. It was also extremely hot inside the skin and he couldn't wait to be rid of it.

All that apart, Pommes Frites had another matter on his mind. Soon after his encounter with the farmer he'd stopped to relieve himself in a most unregal manner through a convenient hole in the skin, and while passing the time by sniffing the ground under the tree of his choice he'd come across a scent which he knew only too well and which meant only one thing—trouble. The trail had led him back to the hotel and there it had petered out, largely because of the difficulty he was experiencing through having a wad of stuffing between the end of his nose and the ground.

For the time being he had decided to stay put, give trail-following a rest, watch points, and await developments.

Some ten thousand metres above Pommes Frites' olfactory organ, in an area where the temperature was well below zero, the newly elevated air mass had started to cool rapidly and condense, while coincidentally, a mere five or six metres below him, Monsieur Pamplemousse, having adjusted to an ambient cellar temperature of 13°C, stood contemplating the contents of a small hessian bag.

As if savouring the bouquet of an old and classic wine, he passed it gently to and fro beneath the end of his nose. It was a cocktail of smells. He could detect thyme, rosemary, mint, verbena . . . a hint of lime, but over all there was a scent which was at once strong, heady, aromatic, woody, elusive. It was like hearing a piece of music which had a dominant theme one couldn't quite place. He loosened a drawstring at the top of the bag, rubbed the contents between forefinger and thumb, then sniffed again. The overriding smell was now even more pronounced. It seemed to come from some pieces of darkish brown bark, dry and curly like old pencil shavings.

'How long have you had this?'

'It's been there ever since Grandpa's day. He used to bring it back from Africa. Mama said he had an arrangement with one of the tribes, but I think they're extinct now.'

Monsieur Pamplemousse couldn't help but wonder if they had worn themselves out. There were worse ways of becoming extinct. Pommes Frites could vouch for that. He must have drunk well that first night. No wonder he'd been in a bad way.

'And it hasn't been used all that time?'

'No, it's been lying there wrapped in tinfoil and sealed with wax. Grandpa didn't come back from one of his expeditions. They say he was eaten by a crocodile.

Grandmère died a little later of a broken heart and after that things were never quite the same. Mama closed the restaurant for a while and by the time she eventually re-opened *tisane* had gone out of fashion. It's only recently become popular again. It seemed a pity to waste it and in Grand-mère's time it was very much in demand.'

'I bet it was!' thought Monsieur Pample-mousse. Perhaps the news had spread as far as Paris and that was why the Founder, Monsieur Hippolyte Duval, had journeyed so far on his bicycle. Perhaps, like Bernard, he'd been an innocent victim of his thirst. In his diary he'd mentioned the *lapin* being over-salty.

'We . . . *you* must have it analysed.'

'Analysed? Why?' The Director's aunt looked genuinely surprised. 'There's nothing wrong with it is there? Besides, there's hardly any left. Only a couple of bags.'

'All the more reason.' He looked round the cellar, wondering what his next move should be. Tell the Director? Keep it a secret? Try and find an analyst first? One of his old colleagues in the Sûreté should be able to help, or at least give him an introduction to the right person. Instinctively he knew he was holding in his hands part of the fortune Tante Louise's *Grandmère* had spoken about so often and yet so vaguely. Perhaps in the end she'd wanted the secret to die with her. Perhaps her joy of life had died with her husband. Somehow, he felt the *tisane* had always been used to give pleasure rather than for any financial gain.

'It's a mess.' Tante Louise misunderstood the look on his face. 'I keep telling myself to get down here and sort it all out but somehow there's never time. I wouldn't really know where to start. I leave it all to Armand.'

He could see what she meant. In their time the racks lining the walls must have held several tens of thousands of bottles, all in neat and orderly rows, numbered and labelled, entered in a book. Now they were in a state of disarray, covered in cobwebs, old wine mixed with new. He put the bag of *tisane* back on a shelf with the other one and took out a few bottles of wine at random. 1950s were mixed with 60s and 70s. Dotted here and there were some older vintages. No wonder one took pot luck in the restaurant. He came across a dust-covered Château Latour '28; its label still intact. Despite being near the river the cellar must be good and dry. He gazed at it reverentially.

It was probably still at its peak—the '28s had needed all that time to come round. Further along he came across a single bottle of Mouton '29 sandwiched in amongst some bottles of Beaujolais. Someone was still doing the buying, but what a waste to put them away without rhyme or reason. He shuddered to think of all the delights that must have been drunk unregarded and un-lauded.

'Would you care to see Grandpa's original cellar?' Tante Louise pointed to a door at the far end, barely visible in the light from an unshaded, but blackened bulb. 'That's where he kept what he always called his *vins du meilleur*.' She reached up to a crevice high in one of the walls and took out a large iron key. As the door swung open Monsieur Pamplemousse caught his breath. For a brief moment he felt something approaching the awe those who first entered the tombs of the ancient Egyptians must have experienced: awe, coupled with an enormous sense of privilege.

There were precedents, of course. From time to time old cellars were discovered; collections of wine came to light. There was the Dr. Barolet sale of Burgundies in the late sixties. That had really been the start

236

of the high-powered auctions which were now commonplace. Then there were the great English collections; ancient families who'd come to realise they owned more wine than they would ever drink in their lifetime. But this was something different and personal. Never in his wildest dreams had he pictured it happening to him. With the utmost care he lifted a bottle from its rack; an 1870 Lafite—possibly the greatest vintage before Phylloxera took its toll.

The first flash of lightning entered the cellar through a glass porthole let into a wall of the outer room. It went unheeded by Monsieur Pamplemousse as he held the bottle up for inspection. Full of tannin, the wine would have taken fifty years or more to become drinkable. It was the product of a more leisurely age. Such an investment in time and patience would be unthinkable nowadays, preoccupied as growers were with stainless steel vats, quality control, and quick returns on money invested.

An explosive crack like rapidly falling masonry sounded overhead as the violent expansion of hot air caused by the lightning manifested itself in a shock wave.

Feeling Tante Louise's hand on his arm he put the bottle gently and carefully back in its place. To drop it would be an un-thinkable crime. 'Don't worry. We shall be safe down here.'

To his surprise she reached across in front of him and turned out the light, then pulled the door half shut. 'Ssh! Listen.'

Straining his ears he caught a faint sound from the other end of the cellar. Someone was trying the door at the bottom of the steps leading from the garden; the same steps down which he'd fled the day before. After a brief pause there was another rattle, louder this time, then a thump as whoever was on the other side put their full weight against it, producing a splintering sound.

'Who can it be? I got Justine to nail it up last night. The lock was broken.'

Monsieur Pamplemousse squeezed in front of her and peered through the gap into the outer cellar. As the door gave way a second flash of lightning, even more vivid in the darkness than the first, momentarily silhouetted a figure in the opening. The face was in shadow, but the outline was all too familiar; indelibly imprinted on his mind ever since he'd encountered it the night he'd arrived. There was the same shopping bag, but this time with a *baguette* sticking out of the top.

Another roll of thunder and with it the sound of rain, sudden and almost tropical in its intensity, muffled the exclamation of surprise from beside him. He gave Tante Louise's arm a warning squeeze and drew her back with him, freezing her into silence a fraction of a second before the light in the other room came on. But he needn't have worried—the intruder had other things on her mind. Going straight to the shelf where he'd left the *tisane,* she took the two containers from the shelf and slipped them into her bag. Whoever it was, she must have reached the same inevitable conclusion as he had.

It was all over in a matter of seconds. The next instant there was a rustle of skirts, the light went out and there was a creak from the outer door as it swung shut again.

'But . . .'

'Wait here.' Monsieur Pamplemousse let go of Tante Louise's arm, switched on the light, and hurried towards the outer door. Halfway along the cellar there was another flash of lightning. The crash of thunder which followed was almost instantaneous, but in the short space of time between the two he heard a familiar and welcome bark from somewhere outside. Pommes Frites was on hand and doing his stuff. Taking the steps two at a time he emeged into the garden and then paused as he absorbed the strange picture that presented itself.

On a bright sunny day Pommes Frites would have presented a fearsome sight; in the middle of the storm he looked positively awesome. The first clap of thunder had nearly made him jump out of his own skin—the second had caused him to split the outer lion's skin in several places, leaving it as tattered as his nerves. With the rain-sodden mane half off his head, pieces of bedraggled fur hanging in shreds and not one, but two tails, he looked like some strange creature created by a latter-day Frankenstein.

Brandishing the *baguette* in one hand in an effort to keep Pommes Frites at bay, feeling in her bag as she went, his quarry backed towards the Sanisette.

Almost at the same moment as she reached it things began to happen in the sky immediately overhead. Negatively charged super-cooled ice crystals and positively charged water droplets, falling at different speeds, were building up a vast potential difference; a difference which in turn produced a gigantic discharge of electricity between sky and ground, heating the air in its path to a temperature five times greater than that on the surface of the sun.

The initial strike path of the flash led straight to the Sanisette, justifying as it landed on its target the designer's foresight in providing an earth return for the protection of anyone unfortunate enough to be taken short in the middle of just such a storm. At the very last moment part of the jagged flash seemed to change its mind and break away in order to complete its journey by another route. A route which took it via the figure trying desperately to unlock the door.

Observers from windows overlooking the square said afterwards, and Monsieur Pamplemousse had no reason to disagree with them, that the *baguette* seemed to glow momentarily before the body was thrown violently to the ground.

Oblivious to the intensity of the rain and hail he hurried towards it, but even as he did so he knew it was a futile gesture; a reflex action born out of a hopeless inability to think of anything else to do. The body lay forlorn and twisted where it had landed. Beside it the charred shopping bag had burst, its contents disintegrating rapidly in the torrent of water which flowed in all directions.

Reaching down Monsieur Pamplemousse turned the figure gingerly towards him, wondering as he did so if he, too, might receive a shock by the very act of touching it.

The right hand was holding a bunch of keys, the left was clutching the remains of what had once been a brass periscope to which pieces of bread from a hollowed-out *baguette* still clung.

The body in its long black dress looked like that of an old woman, but the face was that of Armand.

'Why on earth didn't you tell me?'

'About Armand? You didn't ask.'

Monsieur Pamplemousse gazed at Tante Louise. She was right, of course. Undeniably right. He hadn't asked and he should have done. When someone registers at an hotel you can't really expect the owner to say, 'Yes, of course you may stay, but I have to tell you that the man who does the odd jobs is a little strange—especially when there is a full moon. He has a habit of dressing up in women's clothes, but it has always been that way and as everyone in the village knows, we don't talk about it any more.' On the other hand it would have helped. He certainly wouldn't have taken all those photographs of the *boulanger* if he'd known.

'He kept himself to himself. As far as I know he never did anyone any harm. He was a very simple person.'

Instinctively Monsieur Pamplemousse found himself running his hand over the back of his head. Hitting someone with a brass periscope disguised as a *baguette* didn't sound like the action of a simple person. He could still feel the bump.

'I still do not understand how he could have behaved like that.' Tante Louise sounded betrayed, as well she might.

Monsieur Pamplemousse shrugged. All his years in the Sûreté had done little to further his understanding of what made some people behave the way they did; rather the reverse. In his experience a person with a lot at stake and protecting his territory was capable of anything. Desperate situations begat desperate actions. Betrayal of the one person who had befriended him would have been of small concern to Armand.

'There is no such thing as a simple person. In Armand's case who knows what went on in his mind while he was working away at his bench. No doubt his old mother kept him here because she thought he would be safe from temptation, but being without temptation doesn't necessarily cure the disease—in some cases it makes it fester and grow.

'I suspect you will find that the visitors you had from Paris that time—the ones who made you an "offer"—didn't go away totally empty handed. They didn't sound the sort who would. They would have tried a different tack. Armand would have come to their notice through a local contact, perhaps even from some establishment in Paris he'd written to over the years who'd kept his name "on file". Your visitors probably made him an offer too—but one he couldn't refuse.'

'What sort of an offer?' Tante Louise looked confused. 'He never wanted for anything.'

Monsieur Pamplemousse shrugged again. The preliminary medical report had confirmed his suspicions. Armand had been deeply into drugs; probably brought on initially by the kind of twilight life he'd been forced to lead, and the people he'd associated with in consequence. No doubt in the beginning Tante Louise's visitors had asked for nothing more than a day to day report on the comings and goings at the hotel—who had eaten what and the effect it had had on them. Hardly an onerous task in return for a regular supply of what had probably become almost a necessity in Armand's life. It was easy to picture the attraction such an offer would have had for him. No doubt they even provided plans of the Sanisette.

It was when his masters became impatient at the lack of progress that the trouble would have started; the cutting off of supplies would have triggered off a series of desperate measures of which breaking into the *pharmacie* would have been but one. There was no doubt in his mind that Armand had been responsible.

His own arrival on the scene could only have added to Armand's feeling of panic, but he decided not to say anything about that to Tante Louise for the moment for fear of further questioning.

'It is best forgotten about. Anyway, there are more important things. There is the future to think of.' As he spoke he allowed his gaze to wander round the office. It was the first time he had been in there. On top

245

of a bureau in one corner he noticed yet another picture of Tante Louise's grandfather, taken when he was much younger, the game more modest. He was standing outside the hotel holding aloft a brace of pheasants. Alongside him was a well-built, fair-haired girl, wearing a beautifully serene and yet slightly provocative smile. She looked full of the joy of life, like a ripe peach, lusty and full of juice.

'That was Grandmère. It was taken soon after they got married. She was on the stage in Paris—a dancer in a cabaret, but she gave it all up to come and live here.'

Lucky *Grandpère!* There would have been great celebrations when he arrived back from the big city with his capture. They must have had many friends visiting them in those days; even more when rumours of the *tisane* began to spread.

Standing nearby was another, more recent photograph. Black and white instead of sepia. The subject looked very familiar. It was the eyes more than anything. The eyes and the hands.

'That's Jean. He owns the *boulangerie* opposite.' Tante Louise blushed as she caught his look. 'It was taken before he grew his beard.'

'If you ask me,' said Monsieur Pample-mousse, 'that is someone else who also be-haves strangely. There was a time when I suspected him of being up to no good.'

'Jean? He wouldn't hurt a fly. His only problem is jealousy. He is always on at me to marry him and when I say "no" he gets very gloomy. The quality of his bread goes down. You won't believe this but once, when someone was staying here and he sus-pected their motives, he let down all their tyres. There was a terrible scene.'

Monsieur Pamplemousse tried his best to look surprised. 'Why don't you marry him? It would seem an ideal arrangement and it would make life easier for your guests. It might also improve the cooking. Cooking for love is a sure recipe for success.'

The blush deepened. 'Jealousy is one thing, but I couldn't marry a man with a beard.'

Monsieur Pamplemousse looked at his watch. It was almost ten o'clock. The day before, after the ambulance and the police and everyone else had been and gone he'd retired to his room and slept as he couldn't remember ever having slept before, deeply and solidly and satisfyingly. Now he felt refreshed and hungry.

'Could you conquer your dislike of beards long enough to order me some croissants and a brioche or two?' he enquired. 'I'll be down in about thirty minutes.'

Apart from food, a bath was what he needed most of all. Considering his insistence on having a room with a bath he'd made precious little use of it since he'd arrived. Now he would make up for it. A good, deep, long bath, followed by a leisurely breakfast. Fresh orange juice, rolls, coffee, croissants, brioche, *confiture* . . . as he stood up he caught sight of his reflection in a mirror . . . and a shave. The face poking out of the top of the dressing gown definitely needed a shave.

'I'll see if I can find Justine. I think she is avoiding me—and with good reason. She knows my feelings about people who try to sell "their story" to the newspapers. I have told her—if she does then we are finished.'

'I couldn't marry a man with a beard.' Monsieur Pamplemousse repeated the words to himself as he slowly climbed the stairs to his room, and as he did so he gave an inward sigh of compassion for all the people in the world who were prepared to sacrifice years of possible happiness because they lacked the ability to discuss even the simplest facts of life. It was all a matter of communication.

Tante Louise was more than ready to take up the cudgels on behalf of someone else whose privacy she thought was being invaded, but she couldn't do it on her own behalf for fear of being thought rude, a violator of another's privacy herself. He'd been about to offer her a more up-to-date photograph. He had thirty very good likenesses, but unfortunately all with beards. It would have been rubbing salt into the wound.

As for the *boulanger* himself—whoever said no man is an island was talking nonsense. All men were islands; some allowed in more tourists than others.

Pommes Frites jumped to his feet as Monsieur Pamplemousse entered the room. Fully recovered from his ordeal in the storm, he wagged his tail with pleasure as he followed his master across to the balcony.

Outside the clearing up operations were well under way. Shopkeepers were putting sodden mats on the pavement to dry, washing floors and wringing their mops as if trying to squeeze out the memory of both the storm and its solitary casualty. A van was parked alongside the Sanisette and two men were poring over a circuit diagram, scratching their heads as they tried to restore it to working order. Others were dismantling the scaffolding tower, coiling up camera cables into neat figures of eight as they went. The rest of the media seemed to have disappeared. Put to flight by Pommes Frites, routed by the storm, they were probably miles away by now, devoting their minds and talents to other things. There was nothing so dead as yesterday's story.

The sky had cleared and the sun was shining, but the temperature had gone down. In the fields opposite the goats were drying out, their beards damp-looking and tousled. Like the sunflowers surrounding them they were battered but unbowed. He wondered idly what they were thinking about as they munched their way through the morning. It was hard to tell with goats; unlike Pommes Frites, who from his behaviour had sensed that it was nearly time to move on.

Pommes Frites, in fact, was beginning to show distinct signs of being difficult again. The moment he heard the bath water running he started scratching on the outer door, looking imploringly over his shoulder, as if willing his master to take him out for a walk instead. Monsieur Pamplemousse pretended not to notice. Turning to face the bathroom mirror, he studiously attended to the lathering of his face.

As he pulled his jaw to one side to assist the passage of the blade a long drawn out howl came from the other room. Pommes Frites was bringing his big guns into action. Well, two could play at that game. The second lathering was accompanied by 'O Sole Mio'. Their voices blended well. The bathroom added a certain mellifluousness to the notes as they echoed round the walls. It was quite pleasing. Perhaps they should team up. He could see the posters. Pamplemousse and his singing dog, Pommes Frites—in concert!

Pommes Frites clearly didn't agree. He peered round the bathroom door hardly able to believe his ears. Had he been less busy on the task in hand Monsieur Pamplemousse might well have noticed that he was wearing the doleful expression of one steeling himself for the performance of a distasteful task. It was the kind of expression a dentist might don as he uttered the classic phrase 'This is going to hurt me more than it hurts you,' knowing full well that the reverse was true.

Turning off the bath tap, Monsieur Pamplemousse reached down and tested the temperature of the water. It was even more tepid than usual. No doubt the rapid cooling of the ground by the deluge of rain and hail had something to do with it. The boiler was probably working overtime trying to catch up.

As he rose to his feet again he became aware that Pommes Frites was regarding him in a very odd way indeed. If he hadn't known him better he might well have been forgiven for thinking that he was poised for some kind of attack. There was something about the way he was standing, back legs splayed slightly apart, body tensed and drawn back, arched like a tightly coiled spring awaiting the moment of release. He dismissed the thought instantly as being unworthy between friends. If the truth be known Pommes Frites was probably doing nothing more than limbering up, practising one of his well known leaps in case he had need of it.

Bending over, he reached across the bath for the cord switch which operated the wall heater. As he did so the unbelievable happened. Unable to contain himself a moment longer, Pommes Frites gave a warning growl and then launched himself forward, sinking his teeth as he did so into the nearest available object. And as he dug his feet in and tugged, the sound of growls and tearing cloth combined with a roar of surprise and indignation in a way which made their previous efforts at a duet pale into insignificance, drowning as it did so the splash of something heavy landing in the water, the flash that accompanied it, the hiss of escaping steam which rose a split second afterwards, and the sound of running feet as someone entered the room.

———10———

A Moment of Truth

'WHAT'S UP? Is anything the matter?' Tante Louise nearly tripped over Pommes Frites as she entered the bathroom. 'I was on my way back from the *boulangerie* when I heard Pommes Frites howling. Then there were a lot of other sounds as if someone was in pain . . .'

She broke off and put a hand to her mouth. '*Mon Dieu!* It is not possible.'

Monsieur Pamplemousse clambered unsteadily to his feet and then froze as he followed the direction of her gaze. The electric fire lying in the bottom of the bath looked unbelievably sordid and sinister.

His blood ran cold. He might still have been touching the tap, or testing the temperature of the water, or even . . . even operating the cord switch while sitting in the bath as he had done the night of his mishap in the Sanisette. It was no wonder that Pommes Frites had been so agitated. He must have been instinctively aware that something was wrong without actually knowing what it was.

'How could it have happened? Did you slip?'

Monsieur Pamplemousse looked up at the wall above the bath. 'I think it was helped on its way.' The screws had been removed and the wooden plugs in which they'd been embedded prized out slightly so that the fire had rested on their protruding ends, needing only the slightest of tugs to release it. Nails holding cable clips to the ceiling had been carefully removed, the cable itself remaining in place through years of overpainting.

'Armand again?'

He nodded. 'I'm afraid so.'

'He must have been crazy.'

He wondered if the thought made her feel better or worse. It certainly removed from his own mind once and for all any faint feeling of remorse it might have harboured about whether or not he could have acted more quickly the day of the storm.

'Crazy and desperate. Perhaps he mistook me for someone else.' It occurred to him as he spoke that perhaps the notebook filled with cryptic writing in his own special code had made Armand suspicious. That and the locked case. He must have felt that things were closing in around him.

He reached down and patted Pommes Frites. To his credit Pommes Frites responded not with one of his 'I told you so all along' expressions, for which he could have been forgiven, but instead rubbed himself contentedly against his master's leg. There was really no need for words. 'Good boy' would have been totally inadequate. The pat on the head said it all; the trust which had been so nearly shattered wholly restored.

As he removed the piece of pyjama material from Pommes Frites' mouth Madame Terminé came into the room.

'Oh, la, la!' She took in the situation at

a glance but passed no other comment. It might have been an observation on the state of the weather. She would probably be the same on Judgment Day.

'If Monsieur would care to remove his *pantalons* I will repair them for him.'

'For you, Madame, I will happily oblige. It may give you material for a further chapter in your memoirs.'

'That was very naughty of you,' said Tante Louise reprovingly as the outer door slammed shut. 'And also unnecessary. Justine has already apologised.'

'Then she can work out her repentance with a needle and thread,' said Monsieur Pamplemousse. Wrapping a towel round his hand, he took hold of the cable, lifted the fire out of the bath and placed it carefully on a shelf away from everything else. The fuse would have blown, but from the look of the wiring there was no sense in taking unnecessary risks.

'And now,' he continued, 'I am about to remove the rest of my clothing so that I can take a bath at long last. I shall be down for breakfast in fifteen minutes.'

As the door closed for the second time he pulled the plug and began helping the dusty water on its way with his hand. Depressingly, when he refilled the bath the temperature of the water started to go up and then rapidly went down again. He was washed and dressed and seated in the dining-room in ten minutes flat.

The croissants were delicious. Warm and light and buttery to the taste. He was half-way through his third when Tante Louise entered carrying a pot of coffee in one hand and his notebook in the other. His spirits rose. Suddenly, without bothering to look out of the window, he knew the sun would be shining.

'The maintenance men found it in the Sanisette and brought it to me. It has your name inside. There were other things too —mostly to do with drugs.' The Director's aunt shivered. 'He must have been taking them even as he watched the hotel through that dreadful periscope.'

Monsieur Pamplemousse took the notebook and thumbed through it quickly to make sure it was intact. The writing danced about like the moving images in an old-fashioned flick-a-book.

Tante Louise looked at him curiously. 'The book you are writing . . . food plays a big part? I couldn't help noticing when they gave it to me.'

257

Monsieur Pamplemousse gave a start. He had forgotten about his book. '*Oui, c'est ça,*' he answered non-committally. 'You could say that.'

Translated into a readable form, the notebook was almost publishable as it stood. One day he might even try. He knew he wouldn't, of course—it would be breaking faith with *Le Guide*—but it was nice to have unfulfilled dreams.

'It is nearly finished?'

'The present chapter is. There are still a few loose ends to tie up. I may do that on the way back to Paris.' Calling in on Bernard would be one such end. He couldn't wait to break the news. Given all the evidence at his disposal Bernard should be home and dry. With luck he wouldn't even have to stand trial.

'It will seem strange without you. So much has happened I can hardly believe you have been here less than a week. I think I may close down for a while. The season is over . . .'

He stared at her. 'Close down? But you can't. Mark my words, your season is only just beginning. The name of the Hôtel du Paradis has been in all the *journaux*. Its precise location has been shown on every television screen in France. People will start to come out of sheer curiosity. They will bring their cameras and they will take photographs of the square and of the cellar steps where only two days ago I was ravaged. They will take pictures of the Sanisette. Then they will almost certainly wish to stay here in the hotel.

'It will be like St. Marc in Brittany, where Monsieur Hulot took his famous holiday. Thirty years later people still go there and ask if they can sleep in "his" room. Human beings get a vicarious pleasure out of reliving these things. You will have to engage a chef, of course. You cannot carry on as you are.'

'A chef! I cannot afford one.'

'Nonsense! You are sitting on a fortune.'

'But that is no longer so. If what you say is true it has been washed away in the storm. By now it will be well on its way to the sea. Anyway,' Tante Louise pulled a face, 'I could not have made money out of Grand-mère's *tisane*. It would not have been right.'

Monsieur Pamplemousse wetted his finger and dabbed at some lumps of crystallised sugar that had fallen from his brioche. 'I am not talking of the *tisane*. I am talking of the wine you showed me. A lot of it is pre-

Phylloxera—bottled before the turn of the century. I know someone who would help and advise. Someone you could trust. He owes me a favour.'

That would be another matter to talk over with Bernard. Given his contacts in the trade he was sure to help.

'If you auction only half of it in London or New York it will pay for a new kitchen. You can have the hotel rewired, install new plumbing and heating. Paint the outside.'

He licked his finger again and wiped it dry with the serviette. 'Grandpa would not be pleased if his precious wine was left so long it became undrinkable. That would be a tragedy—to see such an expenditure of love and care and time turn to vinegar. It would have him turning in his grave.' He nearly said turning in his crocodile, but thought better of it.

'Besides,' he brushed some crumbs from his jacket as he rose from the table, 'as far as a chef is concerned, I know of someone who would be eminently suitable. She cooks like a dream and it is time she branched out. You will be doing many people a favour if you take her on. You will have to watch her puddings from Yorkshire—they will not go well with the *noisettes de porc aux pruneaux,* but I think I can safely say that I have only to give the word and she will be here. Who knows? One day you may have a star in Michelin, a toque in Gault Millau, or even a Stock Pot in *Le Guide!'*

He was whistling as he made his way back up the stairs. It was always pleasant when things worked out for the best. He wanted to telephone the Director straight away to tell him the good news—put in some groundwork before annual increment time, but prudence dictated otherwise. He'd managed to escape too many questions so far.

His pyjama trousers were neatly laid out on the bed, folded for packing this time, not for sleep. On top of them was a small square parcel wrapped in brown paper and tied with string. He decided to open it later. Now that he had set the wheels in motion all he wanted was to get away as quickly as possible.

The Director's aunt was waiting for him behind the desk in the entrance hall as he came down the stairs with Pommes Frites. She had another parcel. This time it was unmistakably bottle shaped.

'It is for you. A present from Grandpa.'

He hardly knew what to say. 'You are

very kind. I shall think of you when I drink it.'

'I hope you will come back soon.'

'That would be nice.' Even as he uttered the words he knew he wouldn't be back for some while. One day, perhaps. The integrity of *Le Guide* had to be preserved at all costs. It wouldn't do for Elsie to recognise him. Next time it would be someone else. Perhaps Bernard would pay a return visit.

Goodbyes said, the luggage packed into the boot, he wandered back into the square. There was time for some quick shopping. Pommes Frites' supply of vaseline was running low.

On an impulse, as they entered the *pharmacie*, he took a bubble-packed razor set from a rack just inside the door. 'I would like this gift-wrapped, *s'il vous plaît*,' he announced grandly.

He felt the assistant's eyes following him as they left the shop. By the time they reached the lane at the side of the *boulangerie* she was standing in the shop doorway.

The *boulanger* eyed Monsieur Pamplemousse and Pommes Frites nervously as they appeared at the entrance to his *laboratoire*.

'Pardon, Monsieur.' He pointed to a notice on the door. *'Chiens* are *interdits.'*

Monsieur Pamplemousse inclined his head in acknowledgement. 'We are not stopping.'

He looked around the room. It was always interesting to enter other people's worlds. The doors to the huge ovens at the back were open; the long wooden paddles used for sliding the loaves around so that they would bake evenly were clipped to a rack on a white-tiled wall nearby, their work done for the day. Near the doorway, where the temperature would be coolest, was the croissant area—an enormous slab of shining marble. The floor below was as spotless as the *officine* in the *pharmacie* he'd just left. He could see that Pommes Frites would not be popular if he left a trail of paw prints all over it.

'This is for you. A small parting gift.' He held out the parcel. 'If you take my advice you will use it. If you do not then I can only say that the softness of your brain is equalled only by the hardness of the crust on certain of your *baguettes* and you do not deserve the good fortune that awaits you on your very doorstep.'

Without waiting for a reply he turned and

led the way back to the car park behind the hotel. It was a very satisfactory end to his visit. One last good deed. Thankfully his tyres were all intact. It would have been a very ignominous rounding off of things if they hadn't been.

As they drove through the square he waved goodbye to Tante Louise once more and then added another wave as he caught a glimpse of Madame Terminé on the balcony outside his room. He wondered how she would get on with Elsie. They would probably be more than a match for each other. It would be interesting to follow the progress from afar. He narrowly missed hitting a car coming the other way. White faces peered out at him. It was the first of the sightseers. He'd been right.

In the fields outside the village the circus was packing up to leave. He was just in time to miss the first of the huge pantechnicon lorries revving noisily as it tried to haul its load of trailers through the muddied entrance.

It was a pity in a way they were leaving. He felt a little *en fête* himself. It was a long time since he'd done so many good deeds at one and the same time. Tante Louise, the *boulanger*—if he had the nous to follow his advice, the Director, the Director's wife, Elsie, Bernard . . . it was an impressive list. He wouldn't have minded celebrating it with a ride on the merry-go-round. It was years since he'd been on one. Pommes Frites could have had a go on the helter-skelter.

Through a gap in the trees he caught a glimpse of the Lie. It looked dangerously high, but already Sunday-morning fishermen were out looking for eels and perch and pike, perhaps even a trout or two. In the Loire itself the season would end on the last Monday in September, but here it would go on until April. No doubt they had their minds on the evening *matelote*—the thick stew made with wine, mushrooms and cream, and laced with croutons. A sprinkling of waders and terns were watching hopefully from a safe distance.

He passed a notice saying BAL TRAP, then a small forest of acacia. At the side of the road a table had been set up, laden with jars of honey. Vineyards appeared with their inevitable *Dégustation* signs, and between them more fields given over to *asperges*, followed by a wood which seemed to be alive with men carrying guns.

A little further on he stopped in a lay-by

near a road junction where a D road crossed the river.

It was the kind of day for a detour. He might even head towards Vendôme on his way to Bernard and continue his researches driving through the countryside where Ronsard had lived amongst the orchards and vineyards, writing love poems which likened the pale skin of his amour with cream cheese, before he eventually died of gout. As he reached past Pommes Frites for the maps he suddenly remembered the parcels on the back seat.

The bottle of wine was beyond his wildest dreams. It was the one he'd taken from the rack in the inner cellar. He resolved to drive more slowly for the rest of the journey. He laid it gently and carefully on the back seat, wondering as he did so who he would share it with. Bernard? It would need to rest for a while after its journey. Perhaps he would save it for a return visit by the Director and his wife; a celebration. Such wine was not meant to be drunk alone. He could hardly believe his good fortune.

The second parcel felt hard and angular. It was a tin. As he tore open the paper he recognised it was the one Tante Louise had kept the *tisane* in. Pommes Frites gave a loud sniff as he prized the lid open, then licked his lips. He remembered both the smell and the taste very well indeed. He had drunk very deeply of both that first night in his master's room when it had been left temptingly on the floor, right under his nose.

Monsieur Pamplemousse held the tin up and savoured the almost overpowering aroma. He would always have good cause to remember it too.

He wondered who had left it for him—Tante Louise or Madame Terminé? If it was the latter, perhaps she was hoping for a return visit. *Tisane* in bed with Madame Terminé; it was quite a thought!

Climbing out of the car, he crossed to the bridge and leant on the parapet while he considered the matter. As a parting gift it must be unique; all that was left in the world. The temptations it offered were enormous. He would lose more than his shoe if he gave some to the Director's wife. One whiff and Elsie would burn her puddings.

He held the tin up to his nose again and wondered about Armand. If Armand had discovered the secret earlier he would still be alive. Perhaps he'd had dreams of escaping from it all. It couldn't have been pleasant spending a lifetime being swept under the carpet; spoken of but rarely spoken to. It was a moment of truth. Perhaps he was holding in his hand the answer to a lot of people's dreams of escape. Deep down, he knew he wasn't doing any such thing—he was simply holding on to a tinful of illusions.

On the other side of the bridge Pommes Frites put his paws on the parapet and peered down at the water as a dark brown patch floated into view, spreading out all the time and growing paler at the edges as it was carried downstream by the strong current. He looked up as Monsieur Pamplemousse joined him. There was no accounting for the way his master behaved at times.

There was a series of plops as first one fish, then another, then a third, rose to the unaccustomed bait.

As they got back into the car Monsieur Pamplemousse wondered if the fishermen further downstream would benefit in the fullness of time. Perhaps there would be a sudden and unaccountable rise in the piscatorial birthrate. He might even read about it in the *journaux*. There would be articles.

Expert opinions would be called on, but they would never guess the real truth.

Two kilometres further on they met a road block. There was a caravan—a Mobile Headquarters—at the side of the road. Two *gendarmes* with walkie-talkies and rifles were standing outside the door chatting. A third *gendarme* stepped out into the road as he pulled in. He touched his cap as Monsieur Pamplemousse opened the window.

'Pardon, Monsieur. We are stopping all traffic. There is an escaped lion in the area.'

'An escaped lion?' Monsieur Pamplemousse tried to avoid catching Pommes Frites' eye, but he needn't have worried. Pommes Frites was pointedly watching a butterfly hovering over the bonnet.

'Has it come from the circus?' he asked.

'They deny all knowledge. They say they have only one lion and he is too old to bother with escaping.' The *gendarme* gave a shrug. 'It won't get very far, but it is said to be enormous. There have been two sightings reported already this morning. If Monsieur was thinking of a picnic . . .'

Monsieur Pamplemousse looked at his watch. 'I was heading for Mortagne-au-Perche, but I am late. I may stop *en route* for a meal.'

The *gendarme's* face brightened. 'In that case, Monsieur, there is somewhere I can recommend.' He reached into his pocket and took out a card. 'It belongs to a cousin of mine . . . he and his wife are just starting up. Be sure to accompany whatever you choose with the *Beignets de Pommes de Terre*. They are a speciality. Made with potatoes and eggs and gruyère cheese—grated, of course.'

'And onions and butter?' Monsieur Pamplemousse felt his mouth begin to water. There was a stirring beside him as Pommes Frites pricked up his ears.

'*Oui*, Monsieur.' The *gendarme* seemed surprised at the question. 'With a pinch of nutmeg and salt and pepper.' He wrote on the back of the card and then handed it through the window. '*Voilà!* Be sure and show this to them. They will look after you.'

'*Merci*.'

The *gendarme* bent down and peered into the car. 'That is a fine *chien* you have, Monsieur.'

'Very.'

'*C'est magnifique*.'

'*Oui*.'

'*Un chien par excellence*.'

'*Par excellence.*' Monsieur Pamplemousse revved the engine.

'I am glad to see he is wearing his *ceinture de sécurité.*' The *gendarme* touched his cap —twice. '*Bon appétit,* Monsieur. And watch out for the lion.'

'*Au revoir.*' Monsieur Pamplemousse let in the clutch. As they moved off he glanced across at Pommes Frites, but he appeared to be studying the landscape on the far side of the road. There were times when Pommes Frites closed his mind to the outside world. It would be interesting to know what went on at such moments. He decided to put it to the test.

'*Une promenade?*'

There was no reaction.

'*Dormir?*'

'*Déjeuner?*'

Patience received its due reward. Pommes Frites turned and delivered a withering look. There were, after all, certain priorities in life. Listening to the conversation with the *gendarme* he'd caught the odd familiar word or two; enough to get the general picture. He'd also noticed his master reach instinctively for that part of his right trouser leg where he kept his notebook hidden; a sure sign that he meant business. There was no need to go on about it.

Suitably abashed, Monsieur Pample-mousse put his foot down hard on the accelerator. He, too, had got the general picture, and really, there was nothing more to be said.